*Flying Start*

Samantha Alexander lives in Lincolnshire with a variety of animals including her thoroughbred horse, Bunny, and a pet goose called Bertie. Her schedule is almost as busy and exciting as her plots – she writes a number of columns for newspapers and magazines, is a teenage agony aunt for BBC Radio Leeds and in her spare time she regularly competes in dressage and showjumping.

Books by Samantha Alexander
available from Macmillan

## HOLLYWELL STABLES

## RIDERS

# HOLLYWELL STABLES

## 1

## *Flying Start*

SAMANTHA ALEXANDER

MACMILLAN
CHILDREN'S BOOKS

*Samantha Alexander and Macmillan Children's Books
would like to thank the riding department at Lillywhites
for lending us clothes featured on the covers.*

*We would also like to thank all at Suzanne's Riding School,
especially Suzanne Marczak, Jo and Vero*

First published 1994 by Macmillan Children's Books

Reprinted 1998 by Macmillan Children's Books
a division of Macmillan Publishers Limited
25 Eccleston Place, London SW1W 9NF
and Basingstoke

Associated companies throughout the world

ISBN 0 330 33639 8

7 9 11 13 14 12 10 8 6

A CIP catalogue record for this book is available from the British Library

Typeset by Intype London Ltd
Printed and bound in Great Britain by Mackays of Chatham plc, Kent

# Chapter One

"We desperately need more money!" exclaimed my brother Ross for what seemed like the hundredth time.

It was the first day of the summer holidays. We were all in the tack room trying to make plans for the future. Ross was stalking up and down deep in thought and looking older than his fourteen years. Katie, my little sister, was putting up a poster of an Anglo Arab and dropping drawing pins all over the floor. I sat in a battered armchair with worn-out springs nursing two of the kittens and trying to think positive thoughts. Which wasn't easy when outside the rain poured down in bucket loads and everything looked soggy and miserable. We had left the ponies in their stables and they were munching at their hay and looking thoroughly bored.

"Yes, but how?" I answered, trying not to sound too irritable and grabbing hold of the black and white kitten who was now clawing his way up my neck. "*How* do we raise money when we haven't even got two pennies to rub together? We can't even afford to have any leaflets printed."

"I know, I know. You don't have to remind me," Ross replied, running his hand through his jet-black hair and looking more frustrated than ever. "But there's got to be a way to get out of this mess – we can't give up now – not now we've come this far!"

We had been running the Home of Rest for Horses and Ponies for several months now. It had been our burning ambition ever since we had rescued our first pony from a fate worse than death over a year ago. Since then we had moved to Hollywell Stables; we had saved another pony; we had run up debts with the local farmer and the vet; we had even had our pictures in the evening paper.

"I've got it!" Katie cried out, jumping off the wooden stool she had been standing on, her eyes lighting up like Christmas trees. "Let's have a circus in the field. We could train the ponies to do tricks and invite everyone to see them."

"Oh, grow up, Katie," Ross snapped at her impatiently. "We need proper ideas, not stupid ones."

Katie was nine years old, dark-haired, elf-like and with lots to say about everything. I was twelve, pony mad and determined that one day I would be a famous show-jumper and ride for England.

"What about a jumble sale or a coffee morning?" I suggested, trying to throw in a few ideas. "We're bound to make something."

"Oh, come on, Mel, not enough to buy all the winter hay. And then there's Sophie's vet bill. And what if we get another sick pony? How do we cope then?"

Sophie was a little Welsh Mountain with a chocolate-coloured coat and three white socks, who we had saved during the Easter holidays.

We had found her standing hunch-backed and alone in a sheep pen at a local horse sale. She had a Lot number stuck on her quarters and we could see that under her long shaggy coat she was desperately thin and infested with lice. When Ross examined her teeth we had discovered that she was less than a year old. We had all winced when we saw a deep and blood-matted wound above her stifle which had obviously been left without veterinary attention for some time. Katie had burst into tears and Sarah, our stepmother, had gone tearing off to find an official and make a complaint. Sophie's wide, frightened eyes had reached out to us and despite having no money and no transport we had bid for her. We had saved her from being bought by the meat man, from being taken abroad in terrible conditions and then from eventual slaughter. But for the one we had saved, there had been hundreds that we couldn't and their hollow, defeated faces still haunted my dreams.

"So, what do you think?" said Ross, jolting me back into the present. He was leaning against the saddle racks and looking excited and smug at the same time.

"What?" I said. "What are you talking about?"

"Haven't you heard anything we've been saying, Mel? A horse show – what about having a horse show in the five-acre field? We could have gymkhana races, jumping, lead rein classes, the full works! We could charge entry fees and serve refreshments and have a raffle . . . What do you think?"

"And have a fancy dress!" Katie shrieked, jumping up and down on the spot and scaring the kittens half to death. "And a Chase Me Charlie, and I can ride Sparky and win all the rosettes."

"Yes, but what about prize money? And where would we get hold of some show-jumps?" I said, thinking practically, which wasn't exactly my nature.

"We could get a local sponsor," Ross interrupted, determined not to have his idea dampened.

"Well, I don't know," I said, even though the idea was growing on me fast. "I suppose there's all the Pony Club people and the local riding schools who would come."

4

"It'll be just like Wembley!" Katie burst out hardly able to contain herself.

"We could throw it all together pretty quickly," Ross said, his brain visibly working nineteen to the dozen, plotting and scheming his latest stroke of genius. "What about two weeks' time?"

"Whoopee!" Katie yelled. "That's my birthday."

"What about Sarah?" I said, hanging on to good sense before it went completely out of the window. "We'll have to ask her first."

Sarah was our stepmother and she had been looking after us single-handedly since our dad had died two years ago of a heart attack. Our real mother lived abroad with her new husband who we had never seen, and the only time we ever heard from her was at birthdays and Christmas when she would send us expensive and totally unsuitable presents.

She had never wanted us – she was too selfish to have children and she was delighted when Sarah agreed to carry on looking after us. Sarah was like a big sister and went along with just about anything we decided to do. It was her idea to move to Hollywell Stables and start a sanctuary for horses and ponies.

"Well, what are we waiting for?" Ross said, grinning from ear to ear.

We all charged across the yard to the back door

of the house, eager to tell Sarah our news. As we ploughed into the kitchen, Jigsaw, our golden Labrador, came bounding through from the hallway with Sarah close behind. I was just about to start talking when she interrupted in her deep commanding voice which I instantly knew to mean something was wrong. We all stopped dead in our tracks and wondered what was to come next.

"I don't know whether it's for real or just a hoax," she said, "but I was on the phone and I heard someone shove this through the letterbox."

She passed a piece of paper to Ross, and Katie and I strained over his shoulder to see what it said.

My eyes nearly popped out of my head when I saw what was written. Katie gasped and Ross said something he shouldn't.

It was a tatty piece of notepaper with a child's handwriting; large, round letters and plenty of spelling mistakes, rather like Katie's. But it was what it said that made us all stare in amazement.

PLEASE HELP ME. THERES A PONY IN BIG TRUBBLE AND SHES GOING TO DIE IF YOU DONT HELP. PLEESE BE AT THE CHURCHYARD AT 7 O'CLOCK TONIGHT.

There was no name to say who it was from, not even an initial.

"If it's a hoax, whoever sent it has got a weird sense of humour," Ross said.

Katie's eyes were on stalks and her mouth had fallen open. I grabbed hold of the note myself to take a closer look.

"It's a kidnapping," Katie spurted out, getting her voice back, and her imagination. "We've got to go to the rescue!"

Her huge hazel eyes were filled with horror and she looked as if she was going to rush off that very minute.

"Maybe it is true." I said. "But then why didn't they fetch us or phone the RSPCA? It doesn't make sense."

"I agree, it definitely looks suspicious," Sarah said, turning round to face us. Her long red hair was tied back in a pony tail which always made her look incredibly young. She was still wearing her reading glasses and her small freckled nose kept twitching as it always did when she was being serious – which wasn't very often.

"It's a prank," Ross stated, wiping his hand across his chin where Jigsaw had slobbered all over him.

"But what if it isn't?" I answered.

"Of course, we'll have to check it out," Sarah said, more to herself than to us. "We wouldn't be much of a sanctuary if we didn't do that."

"Hear, hear," Ross answered and I nodded my head in agreement.

"But let's keep it to ourselves for the moment, there's no point phoning the vet or the RSPCA until we're sure of the facts."

"We could get the spare stable ready just in case," I suggested. Already visions of a pony lying somewhere starving and in pain started to fill my head. I had read reports of ponies having to be put to sleep because they were too badly neglected to be saved. My mouth felt suddenly dry and I prayed that this pony wouldn't be one of them.

"What if . . ." Sarah started to say.

"What?" we all shouted together.

"What if whoever sent the note feels frightened or threatened by something . . . What if they want to stay anonymous?"

"Well, why not just tell us where the pony is?" Ross answered, sounding irritated. "If you ask me the whole thing is a farce."

"You don't know that for sure," I snapped, angry that he wouldn't take it more seriously.

Sarah was staring into space and looking thoughtful. Katie was having her face licked by Jigsaw who had at last got someone's attention. Suddenly there was a loud banging on the front door and we all nearly jumped out of our skins.

"It's them, it's them!" Katie screamed out, the colour draining from her tiny face.

Ross looked shaken and I just froze to the spot. The banging came again – louder and more urgent. The house seemed deadly silent and we could practically hear each other breathing. Minutes seemed to go by and then Sarah moved towards the hallway.

"Cooee!" someone shouted through the letter-box. "Anyone at home?"

It was Mrs McMillan. With all the excitement we had totally forgotten about her daughter's pony. I ran after Sarah and saw the estate car and trailer parked in the driveway. They were bringing over the pony to graze in our field for the next few weeks. It was some extra money and we had got more than enough grass. Half an hour later Fenella, a 13.2 Palomino show pony was making friends with Sparky and Bluey and squealing like a young filly.

The rest of the afternoon flew by and we hardly had time to think anymore about the mystery note. Apart from Katie who was treating it all like a Sherlock Holmes adventure. I bedded down the spare stable and filled a water bucket and Ross went with Sarah to get some more horse nuts from the local supplier. All thoughts of the horse show had been temporarily forgotten.

By the time we had sorted out the ponies for the night and devoured the fish and chips which Sarah had bought from the next village, it was time to go. A quarter to seven. We all piled into the old Volvo and set off down the road towards the tiny churchyard. Jigsaw had been allowed to come along for moral support. Ross sat in the front with Sarah who was wrestling with the gearstick and cursing under her breath. Katie was still nursing her swollen finger where Fenella had bitten her and I was counting the minutes ticking by on my watch. We had thrown a headcollar and leadrope into the boot, just in case.

The rain was starting to ease off and the sun was poking through the heavy clouds. Sarah switched off her windscreen wipers and turned up Lantern Lane where the church was set back on the right-hand side. We pulled into a small clearing under some beech trees and turned off the engine. There was no one in sight. Two minutes to seven.

"What now?" Ross asked, still believing that it was all a hoax.

"Let's go round the back to the graveyard," Sarah suggested, opening the door. "The note did say the churchyard, didn't it?"

We left Jigsaw behind and squeezed our way through a tiny wicket gate which was hanging off its hinges. Some sheep were quietly grazing among the headstones and one or two looked up as we approached. One minute past seven. Still no one around. Katie held on to Sarah's hand and we all stood there not knowing what to expect. The only sound was raindrops falling off the trees and the occasional sheep bleating. I felt as if eyes were watching us everywhere. Ross decided to have a look around. Perhaps someone had left another note. Sarah put her arm around Katie and we carried on waiting. A quarter past seven. Ross appeared from behind the church.

"Nothing," he shouted as he walked over to where we were standing. "We've been set up."

We carried on waiting until eight o'clock and now the church didn't seem half as scary. We walked round some of the headstones looking at the names and dates and Katie tried to catch one of the sheep.

"OK, back to the car," Sarah bellowed, deciding we had been there long enough.

"Yippee!" Katie screeched and went tearing off down the path. We climbed into the car where Jigsaw had been sitting patiently on the back seat. I took one last look as we headed off towards home.

"I knew it all along," Ross said in his I-was-right-voice. "If I could just get my hands on who-ever sent that note."

"Well, it's done with now," Sarah said. "We might as well forget it."

It was a beautiful summer evening. Everything felt fresh and alive and a huge rainbow arched over the surrounding hills, vivid and colourful. I didn't feel quite so disappointed.

We had come round in a circle which meant we were approaching Hollywell Stables from the opposite direction. Straight out of the blue, almost like a vision, a horse was galloping alongside us. It was in a field next to the narrow road and was racing flat out keeping pace with our car and with just the stone wall between us.

"Take a look at that," Ross said with excitement as we all strained our heads to get a better view.

"Stop the car, stop the car!" we shouted to Sarah who was bumping along half on the grass verge unable to take her eyes off the horse.

"I wonder who it belongs to?" she said, pulling into a gateway and switching off the engine.

"I've never seen it before," I said, staring at the brown and white body pounding along like a racehorse. It was a skewbald. About 14.2 hands. Obviously part thoroughbred – but there was a stockiness about it that I couldn't quite place. It veered off into the middle of the field and swirled round, snorting and watching us suspiciously.

"It's upset about something," Sarah commented. "Perhaps it's only just arrived."

"It doesn't look very old," Ross added.

"About four or five," I said.

Suddenly it reared right up and waved its front legs in the air.

Without warning it came down on all fours and shot off across the field. Its long tail streamed out like a banner behind it and it was neighing to another horse which appeared in an adjoining field.

"Blimey! It's going to jump!" Ross panicked as the horse headed straight for the stone wall which separated it from the other horse.

"Oh, no!" Sarah said. "It'll kill itself!" The wall was at least five feet high and the slightest mistake would cause a crashing fall. Sarah put her hand over her mouth and I wanted to close my eyes but they wouldn't shut.

The powerful hindquarters bunched together and I could see the horse judging its stride, sitting back on its hocks, checking its pace. One, two, three and it launched itself into the air. For one awful moment I thought it wasn't going to make the height. But then it snapped up its forelegs and soared up and over, landing in a perfect arch and cantering away as if nothing had happened.

Ross let out a long, slow whistle. I gave a sigh

of relief and unclenched my hands. My heart was still hammering. We stood there in silence trying to take in what we had just seen.

A dark figure approached the field from a nearby house and went across to the skewbald, slipping on a headcollar and bending down to feel at its legs. Whoever it was must have seen the jump too.

"Come on, gang. The show's over," Sarah said, herding us back into the car.

"Mel's gone into a trance," Ross teased, grinning at me and knowing exactly what I was thinking. "Wembley wouldn't be so far off with a horse like that, would it?" he said, winking and nudging my arm.

"Ross, leave her alone," Sarah said. "And let's get back before the neighbours think we've left the country."

That night when I climbed into bed my head was buzzing with skewbald horses and brightly coloured show-jumps. But I woke up at three o'clock in the morning with visions of a little pony lying on its side and gasping for breath. Of a blurred figure looking up at me with huge frightened eyes, trying to tell me something – something important and then leading me off into the darkness. It was just a bad dream. I turned over on to my side and snuggled into my pillow for comfort trying to put everything out of my mind. But I had an uneasy feeling that we had not heard the last from whoever had sent the mystery note, that it was not a prank as Ross so strongly believed. Never though, not in a million years, would I have guessed just what the future was really going to bring.

# Chapter Two

"Judges!" I suddenly shrieked out at Katie who stood grooming Bluey by the water trough. "If we're going to have a Best Turned Out and a Fancy Dress we need judges!"

"And bibs and numbers and a loudspeaker, and what about refreshments?" Katie added, chasing after Jigsaw who had run off with the dandy brush.

"Trophies!" I said, scribbling frantically with my leaky Biro and wondering how on earth we were going to cope. I was perched on an upturned water bucket in the stable yard trying to clean some tack and make a list for the horse show at the same time. So far my clipboard read ... rosettes; secretary's tent; show-jumps; bending poles; flags; buckets; sacks; rope; prize money; show schedules; first aid; portable loos ... And that was just the beginning.

"I want to be a cowboy," Katie stated firmly, as she tugged at the knots in Bluey's tail and I reminded her to use the body brush instead of the mane comb.

"We don't even know for definite we're having a Fancy Dress," I answered. "And besides, everybody will go as a cowboy – it's hardly very original."

I was busy flicking through my special horsey diary, counting the days until the show with growing alarm. We had set a date for 9 August which gave us just about two weeks to get everything organized. Sarah had thought the whole idea was wonderful and had immediately scuttled off to make some phone calls, determined to find us a sponsor. Ross was eagerly tracking down some wooden stakes in the toolshed which would be ideal for marking off a show ring. I realized that I had been nervously chewing my bottom lip. I took some deep breaths and willed myself to stay calm. After all, putting together a horse show couldn't be all that difficult . . . could it?

Suddenly there was a loud screeching of car brakes at the bottom of the drive and I nearly jumped out of my skin. Katie tripped over the grooming box and Bluey whirled his head round, instantly alert and straining on his lead rope. I flung aside my papers and tack and ran a few paces down the drive, my heart hammering and half of me not wanting to go any further. For one awful moment I thought there had been an accident.

"What's going on?" Katie was instantly at my

side, breathless and pale and obviously thinking the same thoughts.

A red sports car had stopped at an angle in the middle of the lane totally blocking the road. A tall, blonde girl and a grey-haired man were standing staring up the lane. They looked anxious and the girl was shouting something to the man. Katie and I watched dumb-founded and I had a feeling something terrible was about to happen. For a few seconds there was a silence and then the girl shrieked out – "Look, there he is!" And she started waving her arms frantically in the air. The man hurried back to the car and started blasting on the horn until I thought I was going to go deaf. Bluey was twirling round and round in circles trying to get free, and Sarah came shooting out of the house in a flap with her hair wet and still lathered in shampoo.

"What on earth?" Sarah started to say as she took in the scene at the bottom of the drive.

Jigsaw was barking hysterically and I grabbed hold of his collar to stop him charging off, and with the other free hand tried to calm down Bluey.

Out of nowhere, the strange skewbald horse we had seen the day before appeared riderless in the middle of the road. The reins to his bridle were broken and dangling and the saddle had slipped to one side. He stood perfectly still, spread-legged and wild-eyed, his flanks heaving and his brown and white coat drenched with sweat. Every muscle was tightly bunched and ready to spring forward at any moment.

"You stupid, stupid horse," the girl screamed out, unable to hide her anger. And without warning he hurled himself forward in the direction of the front of the car.

"Get down!" the girl shouted to the man who was stood motionless by the open door.

"Oh, please, no!" I heard Sarah whisper under her breath as we saw what the horse was going to do next. Almost from a standstill it sat back on its haunches and literally jumped over the bonnet of the car. It was unbelievable. The man dived inside the car for cover and instinctively held his arms up to protect his head. There was a terrible scrabbling of metal on metal as the horse didn't quite make it to the other side and got a hindleg stuck underneath its body.

Time seemed to stand still and I was convinced he was going to break a leg or something equally dreadful.

But then he managed to find a grip and half slid, half dragged himself free and stood in a crumpled heap looking dazed and terrified but still in one piece.

"Katie, watch out – come back!" Ross' voice

bellowed out from somewhere behind us and with all the excitement I hadn't noticed Katie running down the drive directly into the path of the horse.

"Katie!" Sarah cried, starting after her.

"What does she think she's doing?" Ross ran past me and I tried to follow but my legs wouldn't move. If he reared up, or lashed out . . .

"Katie come back," I shouted but she was already walking towards him with her hand stretched out. She looked so small and vulnerable. Ever so slowly she took hold of the broken rein. But the skewbald didn't move. He didn't even try to resist. He was still weak after his fright and his head hung low and defeated.

He let Katie gently lead him up the drive just a step at a time. Ross walked alongside, careful not to make the horse jump.

"Thank heavens that's over," Sarah said and I think we all breathed a sigh of relief.

"Not bad, titch," Ross joked, grinning at Katie who was beaming from ear to ear.

I went to put Bluey in one of the stables out of harm's way and Ross looked over the skewbald for any cuts or grazes.

"He's a rig," I heard the blonde-haired girl saying to Sarah as they joined us in the yard. "He's totally off his head." She was flustered and slightly embarrassed and I noticed there was dust and grass stains on her jodphurs where she had obviously fallen off. At a guess she looked about the same age as Ross.

Sarah was talking nineteen to the dozen and dripping water everywhere from her half-finished hair but she didn't seem to notice.

"OK, gang, I want you to meet Mr Sullivan and his daughter Louella. David, Louella, this is Ross, Melanie and Katie."

"You did quite a job back there, Katie," Mr Sullivan said and I could feel my sister's head doubling in size. Close up he didn't look half as grey as I had first thought.

"Don't you ever do that again, little Miss Foster," Sarah said, giving Katie a bear hug and tweaking the end of her nose.

Louella explained how they had been trying to stop the horse running into the village and on to the main road but she didn't say how he had come to be loose in the first place. I found myself staring at her amazing white blonde hair and wondering if it was dyed or naturally that colour. Mr Sullivan was saying that he would need a new bonnet on his car and he'd just had the shock of his life. Sarah offered them a cup of tea and Louella said she must get "the brute" back to her groom. I undid the girth, putting the saddle back in the proper position and wondering how she could possibly dislike such a fabulous horse.

"What's his name?" I asked, running my hand down his powerful shoulder.

"Colorado. He's just arrived from America by plane. He's only been here a couple of days."

"What!" Ross and I exclaimed in unison, our eyes nearly popping out of our heads.

"You mean you've had him flown in from America?" I couldn't believe what I was hearing.

"It's no big deal, really. And he's certainly not worth the money." Louella shrugged her shoulders as if she had horses flown into the country every day.

"It's my Uncle Will's idea of a joke. The stupid horse is half wild Mustang and he knows I wouldn't be seen dead riding something so common."

"Now, come on, Lou," Mr Sullivan joined in. "Will says he's a brilliant jumper – just because he's coloured and a cowboy horse doesn't mean to say he's no good."

"A real cowboy horse!" Katie had just picked up on what we were talking about. "You mean he's a real cowboy horse just like in the films?" Poor Katie looked as if she was about to pass out. "Wow!"

"You're the people who are running the sanctu-

22

ary aren't you?" Louella said, changing the subject and looking directly at Ross who I could swear started to blush.

It suddenly dawned on me what a mess we all looked. Ross had cobwebs in his hair and Katie was wearing her "I'M HORSE MAD" T-shirt with the huge hole under the arm. I felt self-conscious with my filthy fingernails and faded cut-down shorts. Louella looked so sophisticated and grown up.

"We've only just started," Ross said, shifting his feet and keeping his eyes lowered. "We've got the two rescued ponies, Sophie and Bluey and then Sparky who we've had for years."

"But we've got no money," Katie blurted out and I could have gladly throttled her then and there.

"We've got to do some fund-raising," I said quickly and Sarah went on to tell them about Sophie's vet bill and how many bales of hay we used in the winter. Mr Sullivan said that perhaps they could help and Louella dropped hints that it was time she was getting home.

By now Colorado had stopped shaking and was quite relaxed. I offered to help Louella lead him back and she gratefully accepted. Katie invited herself along but Ross said he had things to do although I couldn't think what. Mr Sullivan asked Sarah if he could have a word in private but first he had better do something about his car.

"So which was the roan pony in the yard?" Louella asked as we led Colorado on to the verge to avoid some people out walking their dogs. I was dying to ask her about her own horses but I couldn't get the chance.

"That was Bluey," I said, wiping the palms of my hands on the back of my shorts. It was getting hot and I was gasping for a cool drink. I started to tell her about Bluey. How we had found him being dragged up and down the tarmac road of a council estate by two young girls who thought ponies were like bikes and you could ride them into the ground; his unshod hoofs so sore that he could only hobble and had to keep shifting his weight from one foreleg to another.

How he had been kept in a garage with no sunlight or bedding and given water from a seaside bucket once every few days because the young girls couldn't carry a large bucket of water from the kitchen to the garage. How he hadn't been mucked out for months and his coat was clogged with stable stains and the only food he had was scraps of bread and potato peelings. An expensive present for two young girls who were pony mad and their parents hadn't known any better. They were both out at work all day and they hadn't noticed the

24

pony getting thinner, or at least that was their excuse.

We had brought him home. We had nursed him, sat with him, loved him until he finally started putting on weight. We had won his confidence and he had become part of the family. That was over a year ago and now he looked like any other pony approaching twenty. We had called him Bluey because of his wall-eye which had a pale blue pigment instead of the usual brown colouring. Many people when they first saw him thought that he was blind in that eye but he could see perfectly well – it is just something that some ponies are born with.

By now we had turned into Louella's drive and passed underneath a stone arch which led into the stable yard.

"Take a look at that!" Katie said, bursting with excitement as we were confronted with the most beautiful stable block I had ever seen. Two horses had their heads hanging over the wooden doors and they neighed when they saw Colorado.

"Blake!" Louella shouted, immediately taking charge and marching across to the stables.

A tall dark-haired boy came out of a building with huge wooden doors and carrying a full haynet. He dropped it as soon as he saw Louella and came across to where we were waiting.

"Put this thing in a stable," Louella ordered. "And don't give him an evening feed, he needs to go on a diet."

I handed the reins over to Blake who looked full of concern for Colorado. He had the same dark hair and brooding eyes as Ross but he was taller and not quite so broad in the shoulders.

He led Colorado away and Louella took us across to the two horses in the stables and proudly introduced them to us.

"This is Royal Storm," she said, opening the bottom door to reveal a beautiful chestnut about 14.2 with a blaze and three white socks. His bronze coat gleamed and he was wearing a checked rug with a roller and the initials L.S. in the corner.

"He's a gem," Louella said affectionately and went on to tell us how last year he had won the Junior Championship at the Horse of the Year Show. I would have fallen down from shock if I hadn't grabbed hold of the stable door and gritted my teeth to stop myself looking like an idiot.

"Isn't he beautiful?" Louella said, patting the long sleek neck. Royal Storm shied away towards his manger and Louella eagerly dragged us along to the stable next door.

"Meet the Wizard," she said, standing back so we could admire the finely built bay gelding who was bedded on wood shavings and stood watching us looking nervous and apprehensive. Both his front legs were tightly bandaged, which was odd, but I didn't give it a second thought.

"He's only five, but he's going to be a champion one day," Louella said with conviction. "He's already been placed at the Royal International."

Katie and I stood and admired these beautiful horses and I felt as if we had been thrust into another world – a world of money, success and glamour – and I was fascinated and slightly envious. It was a long way from our scruffy little ponies and make-shift stables and penny pinching to the last pound coin. Louella looked smug, and then she was ushering us towards the house and I noticed that Blake had disappeared.

We went through some huge patio doors that stood open and inside was an indoor swimming pool, surrounded by black and white tiles, expensive cane furniture and sun loungers. A woman was in the pool gracefully doing the backstroke and Louella said this was her mother.

"Why, darling, where have you been?" The woman had suddenly spotted us and pulled herself up the pool steps and draped herself in a towel. She was blonde like Louella and amazingly thin.

"I thought you were never going to come home," she said. "Where's your father? And don't forget you've got to ride Royal Storm – you've got a show on Sunday. And what have you done with that dreadful horse?" Louella's mother looked in the direction of the stables but she hardly seemed to notice Katie or me.

"Yes, mother," Louella said, looking none too pleased and then whisked us outside and round the back of the house to another door which led through to the kitchen. Two little Yorkshire Terriers came tearing towards us and Katie and I bent down to fuss over them. Louella went straight to the fridge and brought out cans of shandy and Coke and diet lemonade.

"Help yourself," she said, beckoning us on through the house. She took us into what looked like the main sitting room and there in a polished cabinet stood a huge array of trophies, plaques and silver dishes, all inscribed with Louella's name and that of the event. One said the Royal Show, another was from Hickstead and another Olympia. On top of the mantelpiece was a picture of Louella and Royal Storm clearing an enormous parallel and in the background was the electronic timing device that you often saw on television and the words the Silver Sable Junior Championship. There was a beautiful red and gold sash which was hung up on the wall and along its length it read "The Junior European Championships, Dublin", and gave last year's date. I felt as if my knees were about to start knocking. For once Katie was struck into silence.

"This is unbelievable," I said, trying to get a grip on myself.

"I know," Louella answered, flopping down into one of the huge brightly patterned armchairs and kicking off her riding boots on to the expensive carpet. "That's what everybody says."

I sipped at my Coke and glanced through the enormous bay window at a tennis court, and what looked like an all-weather riding arena in the distance.

"I've got it!" Louella said out of the blue. "A party! I could throw a party and charge for the tickets and the money could go to your sanctuary."

Both Katie and I looked at her with our mouths open.

"I'm serious," she said. "Next week while my parents are in New York, but you must bring that gorgeous brother of yours. Just wait till Angela sees him, she'll turn green with envy."

Louella's blue eyes flashed with anticipation and I honestly didn't know what to say. "It's all planned then," she went on, hardly stopping to draw breath. "I'll let you know all the details."

At that moment Louella's mother came striding into the room wearing a bright pink jogging suit and huge bangle earrings which didn't look right with her outfit.

"Don't you think it's time you did some jumping, dear?" she said to Louella, throwing Katie and me a false smile. "You can talk to your little friends another day."

I gritted my teeth and decided I didn't like Mrs Sullivan one little bit.

On our way out of the drive, Louella shouted after me, "If you want to have a ride on Storm some time, I'll teach you how to jump."

Whoopee, I felt like yelling, but I controlled myself enough to shout back that I would and "thank you". Thank you very much, I thought, as my heart soared 6,000 feet and my head burst into the clouds.

"That's not fair," Katie pouted. "What about me?" Her bottom lip started to quiver, but I was already imagining what it would be like to ride Storm. Sparky was the only pony I had jumped and we never got further than a simple cross rail.

Back home, Ross and Sarah had faces as long as telegraph poles and even Jigsaw wasn't his usual enthusiastic self.

"What's up?" I said nervously, and Sarah started to fill us in with the grim facts.

"It can't be true!" I said, all my happiness draining away like water down a plug hole.

"I'm sorry, Mel. I know I should have told you before now, but I didn't want you to worry." Sarah stared into her empty tea cup and I had never seen her look more serious.

We had run out of money. It was as simple as that. Dad's life insurance had been spent on buying Hollywell Stables and Sarah was still waiting to sign contracts with the publisher for her latest book. She had been a writer since before she met Dad and she was becoming quite well known as a romantic novelist. What she was waiting for now was the lump sum of money, called an advance, which would pay the bills and keep us going for the next six months.

It was Louella's father, Mr Sullivan who had brought about the sudden crisis. He had offered to buy our five-acre field for a huge sum of money. More money than we had ever had before, but if we sold him our field, we wouldn't have any grazing and that would mean that we would have to close down the sanctuary. It was too bad to even think about.

Sarah was determined to hang on at all costs. She was going to London the next day to see her publisher and hopefully push things along. Ross was furious that Mr Sullivan should want to buy our land and Katie offered to sell her Wendy house and live off bread and jam to save money.

"And there's something else," Ross said, as if that wasn't enough.

He passed me a grubby piece of paper which I instantly recognized. Only this time there was a different message.

I'M SORRY I DINT TURN UP. YOU GOT TO STILL HELP ME. THE PONY IS CALLED QUEENIE AND SHE'S DYING!

There were no instructions for another meeting, and nothing about where the pony was. I turned over the paper but it was blank on the other side. I looked at Ross for an explanation but he shrugged his shoulders.

"Your guess is as good as mine," he said.

"But how can we help if we don't know where the pony is?"

I felt angry and frustrated. It wasn't right that life should be so complicated. What kind of person kept sending notes with such horrible messages? It was cruel, stupid. Irresponsible. I screwed up the pathetic note into a tight ball and hurled it across the room where it landed among the wellington boots. Sarah came round the back of my chair and put her arms round my shoulders.

"It's not fair!" I shouted, feeling the tears welling up in my eyes.

Katie went to Ross who picked her up and she wrapped herself round his neck like a monkey.

"There's just one more thing," Ross said, as if he might as well tell me everything while he was at it.

"I think someone's been sleeping rough in the barn. I found this on one of the bales."

Ross passed me a book that was battered and ripped across its front cover. It was *Black Beauty* and inside on the first page someone had written with a Biro: THIS BOOK BELONGS TO DANNY REEVES. I stared down at the round scrawly handwriting and there was no doubt about it. The child's handwriting in the book was exactly the same as that of our mystery note sender . . .

# Chapter Three

"I don't like her," Ross snapped, dropping a slice of burnt toast on the floor which Jigsaw eagerly gobbled up.

"You don't even know her," I said, slamming the lid down on the marmalade and wondering if all older brothers were so pig-headed.

We were discussing Louella Sullivan. Sarah was hurtling around the house looking for her new pair of shoes and Katie had just turned the stereo up full blast in the sitting room.

"Where's my briefcase? And turn that thing down!" Sarah bawled up the stairs from somewhere in the hallway. Her train was leaving for London at eight thirty a.m. and Mrs McMillan would be here any minute to take her to the station.

She zoomed into the kitchen looking sensational in an emerald green suit, which flattered her red hair all done up in a french plait.

"Watch out!" I shouted as Sarah plonked a stockinged foot in an uptipped flowerpot. The two rescued kittens nicknamed "the terrible twins" had sent the Yucca plant flying and scattered black peat all over the carpet.

"Bingo!" Katie yelled from the doorway, holding up Sarah's new shoes and her plastic four-leaf clover for good luck. Sarah was still hopping around with a soggy toe when Mrs McMillan tooted her brand-new estate car outside the window.

"Now, remember everything I've told you," Sarah warned, clinging to her suede briefcase with one hand and the four-leaf clover with the other. "Any trouble and phone the police and the RSPCA. Mrs White will come round tonight to see that you're all right. Don't go out and don't, whatever you do, try anything silly."

She whirled out of the front door like a gale force wind and we all shouted "good luck" and "break a leg" and then she was gone. Ross locked the door and crammed the remainder of a bread roll into his mouth.

"And before you say anything," he spluttered, eyeing me warily, "I still think Louella is nothing but trouble."

It was nearly midnight when someone banged on the front door. We were sitting up watching a late-night horror movie about a young girl and a ghost with no head. The pounding on the door came just at the moment the girl was about to get strangled. Katie practically choked on a chocolate cream egg and Jigsaw growled and hid behind the sofa.

"Who on earth's that?" Ross asked.

It couldn't be Sarah because she wasn't due back until late the following morning. It couldn't be Mrs White because Ross had telephoned and deliberately lied that we had an aunt and uncle staying who had turned up unexpectedly so there was no need to baby-sit.

The pounding came again, louder and more desperate. It sounded like someone hitting the door with their fist.

"This is stupid," Ross said, and I remembered how we had overreacted before when Mrs Mac knocked on the door.

"Look through the curtain first," I shouted as Ross marched into the hallway. Behind me the grandfather clock chimed twelve o'clock. Katie was holding my arm so tightly I thought it was going to drop off.

Ross opened the door and a draught of cold air rushed in.

"What do you think you're playing at?" Ross shouted, more angry than I had ever seen him. On the step was a little boy, no more than seven or eight. He was so puny, his arms looked like sticks. Tears rained down his hollow cheeks and he was trying to tell us something, something important.

Ross stopped being angry and let him into the house.

"You're Danny Reeves aren't you, the kid whose been sending us those notes?"

Danny nodded his head uncontrollably. I felt a surge of sympathy and put my arm gently around his shoulders.

"Danny, you must tell us about the pony," I said in a soft voice, holding him close and feeling the sobs racking his tiny body. "There's nothing to be frightened of," I carried on. "But we must know where Queenie is if we're going to help."

His eyes looked into mine and some of his fear started to ebb away.

"Sh-sh-she's at a s-scrapyard," he muttered. "You must come. She's got some wire round her neck and she can't breathe."

"I'll phone the RSPCA," Ross said, and went over to the phone.

"No," Danny whispered between sobs. "There's no time, we've got to go now while it's safe."

Ross was already dialling the number. "I see," he said, speaking to someone at the end of the line and then replacing the receiver.

"Apparently the inspector is out on another call

and they don't know when he's due back. They're short staffed and there's no one else."

"Are you sure they believed you?" I asked.

Ross ran a hand through his hair and looked pensive. "There's no point phoning the police," he went on. "They'll think we're just hysterical kids. How far is this scrapyard?" Ross asked Danny.

"A-about five miles from here," he said. "I-I ran nearly all the way, but it took ages."

"There's only one thing for it," Ross said, taking the car keys off the peg in the hall. "We'll have to drive."

"What! You can't be serious?" I said, totally panic-stricken. "Sarah will kill you. You're under-age and what if you get caught?" Sarah's parting words echoed in my head. "Don't try anything silly."

"Mel, this is an emergency. We've got no choice."

The car juddered as we set off into the night, me in the front and Katie and Danny in the back. Dad had taught Ross to drive on an old airfield but he'd never driven on the roads before and not when it was pitch black. The headlights streamed out into the darkness, lighting the way ahead.

Danny was eager to talk now. He was leaning forward on the back seat, his bony hands locked together and his eyes darting between me and Ross.

The scrapyard belonged to two brothers, Bazz and Revhead, who had taken Queenie in part payment for some scrap metal. They thought they could sell her on for a profit.

"It was all right to start with," Danny said. "They t-tethered her on a bit of grass, but then she got ill. She started coughing and her coat went dull and she w-wouldn't get up. Revhead w-wouldn't get the vet because he didn't want anyone s-snooping around and he said it was too expensive. She just got thinner and thinner and I was sure she was going to d-die." Danny's voice trailed off and he stared out of the window.

Apparently Danny lived on the same street as Bazz and Revhead on one of the old estates the council kept talking about pulling down. The scrapyard was out in the middle of nowhere a few miles from his house. He helped out at the yard at weekends and after school and Revhead gave him some money in return.

"But she dint die." Danny carried on, his voice just a whisper above the car engine. "I g-gave her water from a cup, poured it into the corner of 'er mouth and I covered 'er up wi' the b-blanket off me bed. I s-stayed with 'er as much as I could and gave her some porridge oats, but it dint do much good. She stopped coughing but she s-still can't s-stand up right well."

Danny raced on, pouring out his story now as fast as he could.

"And now w-wire's got caught round 'er neck. I knew I 'ad to tell somebody, but they threatened me that if I did, they'd do something to Mum, something really nasty. I read about your place in the paper, but I got scared. If Revhead finds out . . ."

Ross slowed down the car by the side of the road.

"This is it!" Danny shouted, suddenly on edge and as tense as a coiled spring. My heart was beating so loud I couldn't hear what Ross was saying. There was no moon and everything lay in total darkness. We crossed the road and climbed over a metal gate that creaked on its hinges.

"Over here," Danny whispered, moving quickly between old wrecked cars and a burnt-out caravan. Ross switched on his pocket torch, so we could at least see where we were going. There was rubbish everywhere: old fridges, cookers, what looked like a bed-stand . . .

"Here she is!" Danny murmured, bending down on his knees so he could stroke Queenie's head. She whickered with joy at seeing him, but didn't make any attempt to get up. The ground around her was stripped bare of grass and the chain she was tethered to had got caught up with an old washing machine.

"Hold this," Ross said, thrusting the torch into my hand and squatting down beside Danny. "It's all right, sweetheart, we'll get you out of here."

Queenie lay quietly while Ross examined the thick piece of wire which had somehow got caught round her gullet. It was pressing on her windpipe so her breath came in short gasps.

I let the torch travel over her thin little body and felt a stab of horror. Her ribs stuck out like the sides of a toast rack and her stomach was blown up and out of proportion to the rest of her body. There were deep poverty marks down the sides of her quarters, and her flanks rose and fell with every hard-fought breath. She looked desperately fragile and helpless.

"Done it," Ross gasped, leaning back and letting the wire fall loose from Queenie's neck. Her breathing was immediately better and her eyes started to brighten.

She had the most beautiful, angelic face. Just looking at her made me start to cry.

"You poor darling, how could anybody do this to you?" The tears streamed down my face and ran into my mouth so I could taste the salt. It was just like when we rescued Bluey, only worse because Sarah was there to take charge and now the darkness closed in like a deadly fog.

"What was that?" Ross said, instantly tense and on guard. I switched off the torch so nobody could see us. We stood stock still and listened. There it was again. Somebody's voice. Muffled but unmistakable.

"It's Revhead!" Danny whispered, shaking from head to foot.

The torchlights were everywhere. I watched in horror as a huge Rottweiler loped towards us with its teeth bared. White fangs flashed in the darkness and stupidly all I could think of was Dracula.

"Run!" Ross was screaming at us. "Just run! Run!" But my legs had turned into tree trunks and I couldn't move. Ross pushed me hard in the small of my back and then I was running for my life, scrambling through all the rubbish, holding on to Katie and Danny and dragging them towards the car.

"Ross!" I yelled out into the blackness. "Ross!" My voice became hysterical when I looked over my shoulder and saw that he wasn't following.

"Gerroff! Gerroff!" someone shouted behind me. A torchlight flashed and suddenly there was Ross lying on the ground with the Rottweiler towering over him.

"Gerroff when I tell yer, will yer," the youth

with the torchlight kicked out at the dog and it cowered away with its tail between its legs.

Ross scrabbled to his feet and started to run but an older lad caught up with him and grabbed hold of his jacket collar.

"That's Revhead there," Danny spluttered, pointing to the one who Ross was trying to escape from. "The other one's Bazz. Quick, Mel, we've got to do something!"

I picked up the first thing I could find which happened to be a short plank of wood and ran back to where Ross had just been knocked backwards in the scuffle.

"Ross!" I screamed, and hurled it towards him, praying that it wouldn't hit him by mistake. Ross quickly grasped it with both hands and before Revhead knew what was happening, Ross had brought it crashing down on his shoulders.

"Run!" Ross yelled out, as Revhead howled with pain and fell on to his knees.

All four of us darted towards the car before Revhead had a chance to recover. I could hear Bazz shouting something to his brother, but I didn't dare look over my shoulder. My heart was crashing around in my rib cage and I felt sick with fear. What if the car wouldn't start? I dived over the metal gate like a greyhound and Ross swept up a trembling Danny into his arms and bodily lifted him over. Katie was already across the road, but then we had to wait for Ross to unlock the car.

"Hurry up!" I shrieked, tugging at the door handle and trying to catch my breath. "They're coming!"

The car jerked forward as Ross struggled frantically with the gears. "Come on, baby, come on," he pleaded, practically yanking the gear stick out of its socket.

The car shot off down the road. Ross slammed his foot on the accelerator and I instinctively reached for my seat belt.

"Lights!" I shrieked, realizing we had no lights on.

Ross flicked a knob upwards and the road lit up ahead.

"There's no one following," Danny said, peering through the back window and rubbing at the misted glass with his elbow so he could see better. I switched on the interior light and looked back at Katie who was huddled beside Danny and as white as a sheet. Ross was gripping on to the steering wheel with shaking hands and didn't utter a word.

"Ross!" I gasped with horror as the light fell on an ugly, jagged cut above his left eye. Blood was slowly trickling into his eyelashes and he was blinking rapidly to keep his vision. I dived into the glove compartment to find a tissue or something to wipe away the blood.

"I'm all right," Ross hissed as I dabbed at his brow with a duster. The road loomed up ahead and I accidentally switched on the windscreen wipers as I leaned across the seat. We were already miles away from the scrapyard, but Ross was still driving like a maniac.

"Slow down, will you," I yelled, feeling my stomach curling up again into a tight knot. "We don't want to get killed."

The road narrowed dramatically as we turned into a double bend and Ross still had his foot on the accelerator. His jaw was set rigid and his eye was swelling up like a balloon.

"Watch out!" I shouted, grabbing hold of the dash-board as another car appeared in front of us with its lights on full beam. It whirred past us and immediately disappeared round the next corner.

"Ross!" I screamed, as I realized we were reeling into the side of the road. Ross had his arm up over his eyes, completely dazzled by the bright headlights. He rammed his foot on the brake and the seat belt dug into my chest. But it was too late. The car bumped and jolted out of control and then smashed head on into the base of a tree.

*

It was like waking up from a bad dream and realizing it wasn't a bad dream at all. And then the reality starts to hit you and the full horror of the situation takes over.

"Mel, are you all right?" Ross hovered over me.

"Katie!" I suddenly screamed out, turning round to look in the back seat.

"It's all right, she's here," Ross said. "And Danny, too. They're both OK."

Unfortunately, the same couldn't be said for the car.

"It's had it," Ross said, looking down at the crumpled bumper and smashed side-wing.

"Sarah's going to kill us," I answered, listening to the engine hissing and wondering how we were going to manage without a car.

We were stranded on a dark, empty road in the middle of nowhere and every ounce of strength seemed to have drained from my body.

"What now?" Danny whispered, slipping his icy little fingers into my hand. An owl hooted from somewhere in the trees and he shuddered from head to toe.

"We walk," Ross said, trying to hide his exhaustion and put on a brave face. "We walk."

Huddled together, trudging along the edge of the road like a group of refugees, the darkness stretched all around. With no torch and hardly any light from the moon, we might as well have been blindfolded. Every now and then we heard a strange noise which would terrify us half to death. No cars passed but we wouldn't have waved them down for a lift if they had. Ross told bad jokes and we tried to sing songs but couldn't remember the words. Katie complained she'd got a blister and I couldn't help thinking about Louella and how she wouldn't have got herself in a mess like this. I couldn't imagine her with blisters on her feet and lost in the middle of nowhere. I considered telling Ross about the party but decided it wasn't the right moment.

"Queenie – s-she will be all right, won't she?" Danny asked, peering up into my shadowed face as we walked along. I squeezed his hand tighter and tried to look positive.

"Of course she will," I said, deliberately blanking out all my doubts and fears. "Queenie will be just fine."

As soon as we got home, Ross telephoned the RSPCA. The inspector was still out, but he would be alerted as soon as possible and a visit would be made to the premises.

Jigsaw was delighted to see us, but unfortunately, in his boredom, he had chewed up Sarah's best pair of slippers. The kittens had scooted cat litter everywhere and knocked over the milk jug. Ross set about making cups of tea with shovel fulls of sugar which he insisted was the best cure for shock.

Danny looked even thinner under the bright lights and now that all the trauma was over, he barely said a word. I tracked down a half-eaten Toblerone and a packet of chocolate biscuits which turned out to be soggy.

Ross was finally starting to wilt, and I was seriously worried about his swollen eye.

"I don't believe it," he said, looking at his wristwatch for the first time that night. "It's nearly four o'clock in the morning!"

There didn't seem much point in going to bed. Danny had already fallen asleep, so I covered him up with a horse blanket. Somehow the rest of us must have dropped off, because the next thing I knew, the sunlight was streaming through the windows and Sarah was standing in the doorway.

Her overnight bag was slung on the floor and she was staring at us as if she'd just walked into the wrong house by mistake.

"What on earth . . .?" She broke off and gaped when she caught sight of Danny curled up in the armchair.

"I-it's not as bad as it looks," I stammered, still

groggy with sleep and fumbling for my slippers.

Katie woke up, still wearing my old passed-on Puffa coat and bright red wellies. Ross lifted his head from the kitchen table and mumbled "Where am I?"

"Oh my God!" Sarah screeched, as Ross' prize-winning black eye was revealed in all its glory. Ross tried to open his bad eye, but decided it was too painful, and Sarah reached for the nearest chair and collapsed in a heap. She told us how she had managed to get a lift with a friend which was why she was back so early.

"I think you've got some explaining to do," she said, trying to stay calm and looking over at Danny who was still fast asleep wrapped in Bluey's blanket. "I want the full story and I want it now."

# Chapter Four

A few hours later, the RSPCA inspector stood in the kitchen and told us everything he knew.

I couldn't believe it. I wouldn't believe it. It simply wasn't true!

"Are you sure you went to the right place?" Ross asked again for the umpteenth time, searching the inspector's face for any sign of doubt.

Queenie had gone missing. They had searched everywhere, but she had completely vanished. Revhead and Bazz denied everything and said they had never owned a pony in their life. There wasn't a single trace of Queenie to be found anywhere.

"They've moved her," Ross said, pacing up and down looking as if he was about to explode. "The swines have hidden her. They knew we'd ring the RSPCA. And heaven knows what state she's in now."

With that, Danny started to sob harder, and Sarah said that maybe Queenie had got loose and escaped.

"Fat chance," Ross glowered, looking menacing

with his black eye. "That pony couldn't walk across this room, let alone get up and run away."

"OK, OK, calm down," Sarah said, who was far from calm herself. "We'll think of something."

"But what?" Ross screeched, his dark curls flopping forward into his face. "What can we do?" He marched back and forth and tripped over the kitten with the black nose. Katie blurted out that maybe Queenie had died, and instantly burst into tears.

The inspector shifted his feet nervously and looked embarrassed. "We'll do all we can," he said. "But without any evidence . . . It's just your word against theirs."

He dug into his pocket and brought out a card on which was his name and address, and he wrote in his home telephone number. "Call me at any time if you hear something," he said. "I want to catch these ruffians as much as you do."

Just as the inspector was leaving, Mrs Mac popped her head round the door. "It's all sorted," she said to Sarah. "Brian's towed it into the garage. You know you really ought to be in the AA." Sarah made a face and Mrs Mac immediately shut up. We hadn't told the inspector that Ross had been driving and that we'd crashed the car. We just let him believe we escaped on foot and obviously Revhead and Bazz hadn't said anything either. It dawned on me that we still might be charged with trespassing.

The inspector left and Mrs Mac plonked herself down in a chair, only to find she'd sat on one of Jigsaw's Bono's. Her huge bosom heaved as she asked question after question about last night's escapade. I was beginning to wish Sarah hadn't told her. She promised not to say anything about Ross driving under-age and without a licence, although she didn't approve in the least, but then neither did we. She also promised to keep quiet about Queenie. We all decided it was best kept a secret.

I was shell-shocked when she gave Sarah the keys to her estate car and said she could drive Brian's company car for a few days. Brian was her husband. Maybe she wasn't such a bad old stick after all. Then I had to tell her that her daughter's Palomino pony, Fenella, has been kicked by one of our lot and would be lame for the next week. She was not amused.

The house seemed deathly quiet when she had gone, and Sarah looked meaningfully at Danny. The clock on the sideboard said eleven o'clock.

"Don't send me home," Danny pleaded, his small voice a whimper as he looked round at us all imploringly.

His cheeks were still wet with tears and he had dark rings round his eyes.

"Where do you live, Danny?" Sarah asked in a gentle, coaxing voice.

"Twenty-six Riverdale Road," he answered. "W-with me mum. D-dad ran off three years ago with the n-next-door neighbour."

"And what's your telephone number?"

"W-we're not on the phone," he said quickly. "And Mum won't be back till tomorrow. She's g-gone off with her boyfriend."

"So who's looking after you?" Sarah asked, full of concern.

"N-nobody." Danny answered. "I look after myself."

Ross and Sarah exchanged worried looks.

"You'd better stay here then," Sarah said, in her matter-of-fact voice. "So long as you're sure nobody's worrying where you are."

Danny shook his head and looked a little happier.

"Yippee," Katie shouted, and started dragging Danny off to show him her bedroom.

"Wait a minute," Ross said, looking weary and all of a sudden very grown up. He took the battered *Black Beauty* book out of a cupboard and passed it to Danny. "I think this belongs to you."

*

Outside, Fenella banged on her stable door as soon as she saw me. I gave her some horse nuts and changed the Animalintex poultice. It didn't really need changing, but I just had to get out of the house. So much had happened during the last few days that I felt as if we were caught up in a giant whirlwind and it refused to put us down. First the mystery notes, then Colorado, Louella and Mr Sullivan wanting to buy our field . . . Now Danny and Queenie! I felt as if I was on a downhill ski slope, out of control, and nothing could save me. If only Dad were alive. He would know what to do.

But before I could think anymore, a silver Porsche came tearing up the drive and Louella jumped out, dressed in a skimpy sun top, denim shorts and wearing dark sunglasses. Her long, blonde hair cascaded loose down her back and made her look even more glamorous than before.

"Just a flying visit," she gasped, introducing me to her brother Patrick, who was driving and who looked thoroughly bored and fed-up. He turned Phil Collins up even louder on the stereo and tapped his fingers impatiently on the steering wheel.

"Ignore him," Louella said, taking off her sunglasses to reveal heavy eye make-up. "Oh, what a darling pony!"

Sophie, our little yearling filly, had set off at a

gallop across the field with her fluffy short tail high in the air.

"Katie says she'll be a champion one day," I said, as "Sussudio" blasted round the yard and sent Fenella into nervous hysterics.

"What I came to tell you," Louella said, instantly changing the subject, "is that the party's on for the weekend. I'm charging a tenner a ticket."

With all the trauma over Queenie I had completely forgotten about Louella's party.

"Well, you could look a bit more enthusiastic," she snapped, obviously annoyed that I wasn't showing much interest. Before I knew what I was doing, I was telling her all about Queenie. Pouring out the whole story which she listened to with her mouth wide open. It was almost as if all the sunlight had gone out of her face. I thought she was upset about Queenie. But I was wrong. If only I'd known then what she was really thinking.

She left in a hurry, shouting back that she would try to talk her dad out of buying our field. And, like a fool, I believed her.

When I went back into the house, Ross looked more like his old self. Sarah was busy scouring the saucepans with Brillo pads (she always started cleaning when she was worried) and Katie and Danny were playing Monopoly on the sitting-room carpet.

"We've come up with a plan," Ross whispered, his dark eyes sparkling with excitement. He closed the kitchen door so that Katie and Danny couldn't overhear. And then he sat down and told me all about how we were going to rescue Queenie. I listened intensely and my heart started to beat faster. Perhaps there was a way after all.

"You didn't say anything to her, did you?" Ross asked suddenly as an afterthought. He meant Louella.

"No," I found myself lying, "I didn't say a word."

The darkness clung all around. We were huddled in Mrs Mac's estate car, parked down the road from Revhead's scrapyard, hidden out of sight. I was so nervous, my skin tingled as if millions of ants were crawling all over me. Sarah was muttering over and over that she was crazy to be talked into this and that she could be locked up for being a bad mother. Ross tried to make light of everything, but it didn't hide the fact that we were all terrified.

According to Danny, Bazz would be spending the night with his girlfriend and Revhead would be going down to the White Swan with some of his mates for a drink. We had sat outside their house, inconspicuous behind a large removal van and we had watched them both come out; Revhead getting a lift in an old pick-up truck and Bazz roaring off on a black and gold motorbike.

Now was our only chance. If we were ever to see Queenie again – it was now or never. Fear caught in the back of my throat and dried up my mouth. I couldn't stop my hands shaking.

Danny and Katie were sitting on the back seat and I was squashed in the middle. Sarah had argued all day that they should stay behind, but Ross had pointed out that we needed Danny to direct us to Revhead's house and if we didn't take them, we would have to find a baby-sitter and there was no one available – only Mrs Mac, and she would want to know where we were going and what we were up to.

So Katie and Danny were to stay in the car with Sarah. Ross and I were to search for Queenie and as soon as we found her, come back to the car and Sarah would ring the RSPCA. Luckily Mr McMillan's executive car had a telephone. Danny assured us the Rottweiler would be chained up by the front gate. If we sneaked round the back it wouldn't see us, and Danny was convinced Queenie was in an old pumphouse right at the back of the premises which the inspector might not have spotted.

It all sounded so simple. All we had to do was find Queenie. This time there was no Revhead or Bazz to disturb us and we had two powerful flash lights to guide the way.

The car door squeaked as I pushed it open and the night air enveloped me. It was a warm, balmy evening, but it didn't stop me trembling from head to toe. Ross held on to my hand and we scrambled through a gap in the hedge which opened out into a large field. We sneaked down the side of the hedge which would lead us round the back of the scrapyard. Already my heart was hammering like a piston and I didn't think I could go through with it.

"Come on, Mel!" Ross tugged at my hand and my concrete legs bundled forward. "Just keep thinking about Queenie," he hissed through clenched teeth.

The ground was hard and rutted and I kept tripping awkwardly in the darkness. My right ankle twinged with pain and my back ached from stooping down to stay out of sight.

"Here!" Ross stopped at a wire fence and shoved his torchlight into my hand. He pulled the top strand of wire up so I could climb through and I immediately stumbled down a steep bank and landed in a clump of nettles.

"Ouch!"

"Sssssh!" I heard Ross' voice behind me. I struggled to my feet and passed him the torch. A dog howled in the distance and I thought I heard a chain clinking.

"Maybe we should go back." I hesitated, my teeth rattling like a road digger.

"No way," Ross was instantly at my side and pulling me across the rough ground towards a dark shadow in the distance.

"This has got to be it," he said, as we edged round a small, isolated building, slowly feeling our way against the rough stone. A loose sheet of corrugated iron creaked and I tripped over a piece of wire. Ross peered through a window, but it was too dusty to see anything. Then he pushed a door open and we walked inside.

The air was clammy and stale, and at first there didn't seem to be anything there. Ross swung his torch back and forth, lighting up different corners of the building. There was a scuttle behind a stack of crates and my fingernails dug into Ross' hand.

"Just a rat," he whispered, and the hair started to stand up at the back of my neck.

Then we heard it.

A very faint whinny from behind a wooden partition. It was barely audible, but I knew straight away it was Queenie. We dived forward and there she was; half hidden behind the barrier, laid down, but not flat out as she had been before. She whickered again when she saw us, a deep, throaty greeting, and her dark, dusky eyes blinked in the sudden light of the torch.

"There's my girl," Ross murmured excitedly, as he bent down to stroke her. "It's OK, we're not going to leave you again."

I ran my hand down her soft neck and secretly thanked God that we had found her. She buried her nose in Ross' pockets and sniffed at some pony nuts which he held out in the palm of his hand. She was definitely brighter and more alert than the previous night, and someone had actually removed the headcollar which had been digging into the soft flesh behind her ears.

"You poor old thing," I whispered, running my hand over her delicate body and thinking how I could count every rib, feel every bone under the taut, dry skin. But it didn't matter. It didn't matter because we were going to take her home. Make her well again like we had Bluey and Sophie. Everything was going to be all right.

"We'd better get back and tell Sarah," Ross said, standing up, and putting the untouched pony nuts back in his pocket. I suddenly remembered Sarah, Danny and Katie waiting anxiously in the car and knew we had no time to lose.

"But what about Queenie?" I said. "We can't both leave her."

"Mel, if Revhead or Bazz come back and find us we're dead meat. We've got to phone the RSPCA and let them deal with it."

Ross was right of course, but I hated having to desert Queenie for a second time.

I was the first to move past the wooden partition towards the doorway. And there I stood, frozen with terror, as the huge bulk of Revhead loomed in the doorway.

A terrible sick feeling gripped my stomach, and I stood there for what seemed a lifetime reeling with disbelief and growing panic.

Revhead stared back at me; his pulpy, marshmallow face breaking into a cruel and sadistic grin.

"Thinking of going somewhere are you?" he leered, leaning back against the door frame and enjoying every minute of my discomfort.

"To the police for starters," Ross' voice thundered out behind me, stony and menacing as I had never heard it before.

"Is that a fact?" Revhead sneered, shifting his gaze to Ross, and eyeing him up and down. Ross took a step forward and Revhead sprang into action.

"Not ruddy likely," he grunted, picking up a metal crowbar that was leaning against the wall.

"Let's see yer protect yer little sister now, big brother." And he lunged forward and tried to grab hold of my arm, but I was too quick and his huge hand snatched at empty air. Ross pulled me back behind him and turned to face Revhead.

"There's no one to bully now, is there?" Ross said, and for the first time Revhead started to look nervous. "That's how you get your kicks is it?" Ross went on taunting him. "Bullying kids and helpless animals. Well come on," he beckoned, snarling at Revhead like a maddened animal. "See how it works on me. Come on, you big oafhead!"

Revhead leapt at Ross, swinging the crowbar high in the air. Ross dodged to one side and managed to give Revhead a cracking blow in the ribs. Revhead screamed with rage and charged at Ross again.

"Come on, you scumbag!" Ross jeered, as Revhead went crashing into an old lawnmower.

My heart clenched with fear.

Revhead was twice the size of Ross. I didn't know whether to run for help, or try to hit Revhead with something heavy – but they were both moving so fast – what if I hit Ross instead?

Queenie was neighing frantically and I heard her trying to scrabble to her feet. Revhead was lunging towards Ross again. There was hardly any room for Ross to escape. Revhead lifted the crowbar. Ross jerked to one side, but somehow his foot got wedged and he lost his balance. I screamed out to warn him, but he couldn't move out of the way fast enough. Revhead brought the crowbar hurtling down across his left arm. I was convinced I heard something crack. Ross' face contorted in agony. His left arm hung limp and lifeless, and beads of sweat ran down his face.

And I was running too – running as hard as I could, out in the night air, back to the wire fence and the gap in the hedge that would lead me to the car and Sarah. My breath came ragged, my chest ached and my legs grew heavy. I must fetch help. I must fetch help.

"Mel! . . . Mel!" A familiar voice rang out in the darkness.

A torchlight flashed and a wave of relief flooded over me. It was Sarah.

"Where's Ross?" she asked, running up to me in her multi-coloured trainers which glowed like beacons in the dark. Anxiety was etched all over her face.

I tried to tell her, but the words got stuck in my throat. I could only drag her back the way I had come. Back to Ross and Queenie . . . and Revhead, who had probably killed them both by now.

We reached the old pumphouse and flung open the door. Sarah gasped with horror. I stared in amazement. Revhead lay unconscious in a crumpled heap by the stack of crates. His legs and arms splayed in all directions, as lifeless as a rag doll. Ross was propped up against the wall, nursing his injured arm and looking battered and beaten. Queenie was up on her feet, swaying slightly, but standing over Ross as protective as a dog. It was like a scene from an old cowboy movie and any minute now I expected John Wayne to walk in behind us.

Relief spread over Ross' face and he tried to grin, but it turned into a grimace.

"What took you so long?" he said, and then his knees buckled and he slid down the wall.


The next few hours were confused and chaotic. Sarah had already rung for the police as soon as she saw Revhead arrive at the scrapyard. Now two policemen were looking around the pumphouse and asking hundreds of questions.

Ross and Revhead were bundled off to casualty, Ross with a suspected broken arm and Revhead with concussion. Sarah had gone with them, which left me to explain everything to the police. The younger one with ginger hair kept chewing the end of his pen and repeating the same questions. Katie and Danny gawped with their eyes on stalks and Katie asked me if we were going to be arrested.

The RSPCA inspector and a vet came to examine Queenie and said they thought she was going to be all right. Queenie nuzzled at Danny's shoulder affectionately and I was suddenly overwhelmed with tiredness and had to sit down.

"What did you say your place was called?" The vet was leaning over me with enquiring eyes.

"Hollywell," I mumbled, my jaws aching with exhaustion. "Hollywell Stables."

"Sanctuary for Horses and Ponies," Katie blurted out proudly, and then sleep dragged at my eyelids and that was the last thing I remembered.

# Chapter Five

Queenie arrived at Hollywell in the early hours of the morning.

She stumbled out of the borrowed horsebox into one of the stables and it took all the inspector's and the vet's strength to keep her from falling down. Danny refused to leave her and Katie kept asking if she was going to be all right which only made things worse. Sarah came back from the hospital with Ross who had his arm in plaster. She took one look at everybody's weary faces and went straight inside to make mugs of tea.

Queenie looked even thinner under the bright fluorescent light, and the vet gave her an injection which he said would act as a booster. He was a kind-looking man with soft brown eyes and gentle hands and he insisted we called him James.

"So what now?" Sarah asked when she reappeared from the house carrying the mugs of tea and looking bleary eyed and exhausted.

"We'll prosecute," the RSPCA inspector answered, rubbing a hand over his stubbly chin and smothering a yawn. It had been a long night. "We'll have Revhead up in court for cruelty through negligence, but it'll be months before it comes in front of the magistrates. And then he'll only get a fine of, at the most, two hundred pounds."

"But he will be banned from keeping any more horses, won't he?" Ross asked, leaning over the stable door with his one good arm.

"For about three or four years, yes, maybe not as long as that. But we'll be keeping an eye on him, don't you worry. One foot wrong and we'll be down on him like a ton of bricks."

"So he won't be going to prison, Mister?" Danny looked up with frightened eyes and I knew what he was thinking.

"Don't worry, Danny, Revhead won't hurt you or your mum. He was just making threats to scare you."

"No, laddie," the inspector added. "He won't go to prison, but I should think the police will be more than interested in his scrapyard. If you ask me, Revhead will be up to his neck in trouble."

"Let's hope so." Sarah shuddered and passed round the tea. Katie ripped open a packet of Jammy Dodgers and everyone realized they were starving.

"What about Queenie?" I suddenly blurted out

with my mouth full, worried about how we stood with the law. "Will we be able to keep her?" Before we had bought both Bluey and Sophie and this was also the first time we had dealt with the RSPCA.

"'Course you will," the Inspector answered, taking a sip out of Katie's special Desert Orchid mug. "That's your job, isn't it, rescuing poor little mites like her," and he winked at Sarah who put her arm round my shoulder. "It's just a pity there aren't more places like this," he went on more seriously. "Good luck to you, that's what I say."

Right now, I thought, we needed all the good luck we could get.

It was nearly daylight when the vet and the inspector finally left. This was the second night with hardly any sleep and my eyelids felt as if they needed propping up with matchsticks to keep them open.

The vet said he would be back the next day and that we could try feeding Queenie some sugar beet and bran with maybe a sliced apple. Sarah bodily dragged Danny into the house and sent him upstairs with a pair of pyjamas, but to no avail because later we found him fast asleep in Queenie's stable.

Mrs Mac came round bright and early to see

Fenella and demanded to know the whole story. Sarah was still wandering around in her dressing gown at lunchtime when James pulled into the driveway in his blue Volvo. Queenie hadn't eaten anything yet apart from a sliced carrot and half an apple.

"Now then, my little girl," James whispered as he bent down and patted Queenie's neck. She looked up at him with her huge liquid eyes and it struck me again just how beautiful she was. James took her temperature and listened to her breathing, feeling over her flanks and belly.

"And you say she won't touch any food?"

I told James what she had eaten and sensed his growing concern. Ross came in, and together they managed to coax Queenie on to her feet. She was only about 12.2 hands with a little star on her forehead and a dusty brown body. James examined her teeth and said she was well into her twenties. Ross told Danny and Katie to fetch a towel and as soon as they were out of earshot he asked James what he thought.

"At this stage I can't say," he answered, leaning back against the stable wall. "I'll take a blood sample which will tell me all I need to know."

"But you must have some idea," Ross persisted, his eyes fixed on James who looked tired and worried.

"I can't say for definite," James started. "But there's a possibility she may have chronic ragwort poisoning. It's not impossible that she's got some liver damage, but I really can't say yet."

My heart missed a beat and Ross looked shocked. Ragwort is a deadly plant with yellow flowers that are poisonous to horses and it tends to grow on rough wasteland. If a horse was really hungry it would eat it.

My legs suddenly felt so weak I could barely stand up. I couldn't even hear what James went on to say. All I could see were his lips moving and Ross nodding his head and looking grave and serious. It wasn't fair. Not after all we'd been through to save her. Not for it now to be too late. Queenie watched us quietly and looked almost apologetic. I felt like throwing my arms round her neck and I knew I couldn't bear it any longer. I flew out of the stable and ran across to the field gate where Bluey stood dozing in the sunshine. The tears were stinging in my eyes and I buried my face in his thick thatch of mane and wished someone would wave a magic wand and make everything right again. But I knew that wouldn't happen.

Ross came up behind me and put his hand on my shoulder.

"Come on, it's not that bad."

Bluey moved away and I was conscious of my hot flushed face.

"Come on, Turnip," Ross said, clucking me under the chin and using the nickname I had when I was younger. "She's going to be all right. I promise you. Just give her time. But let's not breathe a word of this to the kids," he added. And I knew keeping this from Danny was going to be nearly impossible.

We broke the news to Sarah and she agreed that we must not tell Katie or Danny. James was going to ring that evening as soon as he had the results from the blood test. Mrs Mac was determined to be of help and set about making a treacle pudding which she said would give us strength and fortitude. Sarah said she was a brick and Ross joked that he would prefer a chocolate cake.

Katie and Danny came charging into the kitchen saying they had christened the kittens Oswald and Matilda and would Ross like Jigsaw's paw mark on his pot.

Later in the afternoon Sarah dragged Danny off in the car to see his mother and we all promised him he could come and see Queenie any time. Ross tried once more to get Queenie to eat something, while I went into the next stable to groom Fenella who was furious that she wasn't the centre of attention. I was just brushing out her long creamy

71

mane when I heard hoof beats coming up the drive and saw Louella's groom Blake ride into the yard on Royal Storm and leading the Wizard. They looked so bright and dazzling in the afternoon sun and I couldn't help but notice how well Blake sat in the saddle.

"Hi," he said with a faint smile, patting the chestnut's broad neck and dismounting. The Wizard sidestepped skittishly, but relaxed as soon as Blake spoke to him.

"Lou asked me to give you a message," he started, fumbling with the reins and looking slightly embarrassed. I quickly brushed the loose hairs off the front of my T-shirt and wished I didn't look such a mess.

"It's about the party . . ."

"What party's that?" asked Ross in a friendly tone, coming out of Queenie's stable and looking enquiringly at Blake. I mumbled an introduction and suddenly realized that I'd completely forgotten to mention the party to Ross. I dodged behind Royal Storm's shoulder as Blake explained, and I saw Ross' face harden.

"Well, you can count me out," he said bluntly, causing my face to turn bright purple.

"Ross!" I exclaimed, wishing the ground would open up and swallow me. "It is in aid of the stables. You can't just not go."

Blake levelled a steady gaze at Ross, and it struck me how alike they looked with their black eyes and hair.

"Can't say I blame you," Blake mumbled, without breaking his gaze away from Ross.

But before I could change the subject, a motorbike came roaring up the drive, sending the horses wild. The noise was deafening and it scuffed up a cloud of dust as it screeched to a halt in front of us. There were two youths on the bike, their jean-clad legs straddling the black and gold bodywork.

I knew who it was even before they took off their crash helmets. The bike glinted in the sun like an evil monster.

"What the hell?" Blake cursed as the Wizard reared up and Storm pulled in the opposite direction. The lad in front jeered and laughed in his thick, coarse accent and lifted off his helmet. It was Bazz.

He was shorter and stockier than his brother Revhead, but he had the same pasty skin and cruel eyes. He leered at us and revved the bike up to scare the horses more. I didn't recognize the lad sat on the back who was obviously Bazz's sidekick. He was pimply-faced with a flat nose and a scar across his right cheek. Just looking at him gave me a twinge of fear.

Bazz stepped off the bike and stood across from

us. Ross managed to herd the horses into two empty stables and bolt the doors.

"Bet yer think yer really clever, don't yer?" Bazz yelled, his voice thickening with anger. His fish-like eyes moved over the three of us, cold and stony – ready for trouble. The scar-faced lad took up his position at Bazz's side.

"Can't do much with that arm now, can yer, lover boy?" Bazz went on, goading Ross who started flushing with anger. "Pity we didn't break that pretty face of yours too, eh? What about another black eye, eh? Or maybe yer sister might like one?"

The other youth laughed and Bazz moved a few steps forward, balling his fists and looking threatening.

"You low-life," Ross snarled back, barely able to speak for boiling anger. His one good arm hung by his side, taut and clenched. "Get off this property before I phone the police."

The words hissed out as a threat, and I held my breath as the air seemed to hang still between us. Bazz spat on the ground and the other lad giggled.

"You heard what he said."

The voice was quiet and soft. It was the first time Blake had spoken, and it knocked Bazz off guard.

"And who do yer think you are, Tom Cruise?" Bazz jeered, looking Blake up and down, sizing him up. Blake stood completely still and relaxed, hardly moving a muscle.

"Oh, why don't you just go!" I shouted out without thinking. "You're not getting Queenie back. I'd rather die than let her go back to a toad like you!"

Bazz wheeled round in my direction, his boot heel scrunching in the gravel, his eyes frozen on my face. My heart leapt inside my rib cage as I realized what I'd said.

"You silly little kid," he sneered. "Do yer really think I came here for that useless nag?"

I could practically feel his heavy breath on my face and neck.

"It's yer brother here I came to see," he went on, moving closer to Ross. "Yer see, nobody messes with me and gets away with it. D'yer hear? D'yer hear what I'm saying?"

I felt sick with terror.

Suddenly he made a lunge for Ross' broken arm. Ross yelped in pain and the other youth moved forward, but Blake was quicker. He clasped a hand round Bazz's throat and pushed him back, pinning down his arms with his other free hand.

Bazz's eyes rolled round his head, he was spluttering, half with shock and half lack of breath. Blake's face was set like a sheet of steel. His hand tightened round Bazz's throat and he pushed him back against the seat of the motorbike. The other lad cowered away.

"Now, you listen to me," Blake said. "I don't know who you are and, quite frankly, I don't care. But I don't like bullies. Do you understand me?"

Bazz's head nodded violently, his mouth lolling open.

"Now, get on your bike and take that sponge-head with you. And clear off before I lose my temper."

Blake roughly let go, and Bazz scrambled on to the bike, his bottom lip trembling and his face stark white. The other lad leapt on behind him and they wheeled off. But halfway down the drive, Bazz stopped and yelled out,

"Yer not getting away wi' this. I'll be back, yer won't always 'ave beefcake to protect yer. Just yer wait!"

He shook his fist in the air and then disappeared. I couldn't believe it was all over. Ross was the first to speak.

"I think we owe you one," he said gratefully to Blake who shrugged his shoulders and pretended it was nothing. I for one felt like hugging him to death.

We showed Blake Queenie and explained the story of the last few days. So much seemed to have happened I still found it hard to take in. Blake listened quietly, nodding his head and gently fondling Queenie behind the ears. She seemed to instantly trust him, and nuzzled at his hair as if they were long lost pals.

"I think you've made a friend there," Ross chuckled, and the Wizard squealed in the next-door stable as if he was jealous.

"I'd better be going," Blake said, and moved towards the stable door. "You could try giving her some black treacle from your hand," he suggested, looking back at Queenie. "It's only an idea, but it worked once with one of mine."

"Right, you're on," Ross replied, and we went to fetch the horses.

"About Louella," Blake said as he swung into the saddle. His forehead was knotted with furrows and he looked anxious. I had a feeling I didn't want to hear what he was going to say.

"It's just that . . . Well—" He broke off and looked down at the saddle. "Nothing," he said, quickly changing his mind. "Forget I said anything." And with that he shortened his reins and rode off down the drive with the Wizard lagging behind.

"Well, what do you make of that?" Ross said, watching Blake disappear down the road.

"How would I know?" I snapped back, feeling irritated.

"I'll tell you what," Ross answered in a stern voice, giving me one of his eyeball-to-eyeball looks. "He's hiding something. That much I am sure about. And I bet you any money it's got something to do with Louella."

Sarah came back from seeing Danny's mum looking hot and flustered. Katie had gone along for the ride, but we were amazed to see Danny get out of the back of the car as well. He was lugging two carrier bags, stuffed full of what seemed to be clothes and odds and ends, but as soon as he was out of the car he dropped them down and went running over to see Queenie.

Later, in the kitchen, Sarah told us what had happened. Steam was still coming out of her ears and she shut the back door so that Danny and Katie wouldn't be able to hear.

"Of all the impossible women," she started, wringing out the dishcloth until it nearly ripped in half. "How can anybody treat their children like that? I could have rammed those false eyelashes down her weasly throat. Do you know, she didn't even care where he'd been, or what he'd been up to?"

Ross managed to calm her down before she burst a blood vessel.

"Half the time I don't think she can even remember his name, let alone that he's her son!"

"OK, OK, calm down," Ross said, as Sarah plonked three heaps of sugar in her tea and slammed down the spoon.

Danny was to stay with us for three weeks while his mother went on holiday to Brighton with her boyfriend.

"Heaven knows what would've happened to him if he hadn't met us," Sarah said.

"People like that should be reported," I said, horrified at the thought that Mrs Reeves would have just left Danny to fend for himself.

"And there's something else," Sarah said, holding her hands on her forehead and pursing her lips. "I ran into David Sullivan at the village shop. He's pushing for an answer about the field. Wants to know for definite by next week. I mean, can you believe it?"

I plopped myself down in the armchair with Oswald and Matilda. Why did life have to be so difficult? Ross and I had agreed not to tell Sarah about Bazz's little visit and, looking at her now, she seemed to have enough on her plate to worry about. I had never seen Sarah so rattled and wound up. Usually she was a pillar of strength and seeing her like this made me feel strangely vulnerable. I tried not to think about our money problems, but it was hopeless.

"I don't see that I have a choice," Sarah went on.

"If nothing's happened by next week I'll have to agree to sell."

Please, dear God, let something happen, I found myself thinking, and cuddled little Matilda closer for comfort.

Waiting for James' phone call was a nightmare. The hours seemed to drag by and it was exhausting trying to pretend to Katie and Danny that nothing was wrong. Mrs Mac took her daughter for a ride on Fenella who was now fully recovered. And she also took it on herself to organize the horse show. Already she had ordered the rosettes and got most of the equipment together for the gymkhana races, including the sacks and the bending poles. We were all seriously impressed, not to mention relieved. Mrs Mac, or Gladys as Sarah called her, seemed to have a natural ability for organizing. In fact, she reminded me of a Sergeant Major.

It wasn't surprising that, with all the strain, Ross and I had an argument. It all started over Louella's party. I was determined not to give in.

"I'm going whether you like it or not," I screamed at the top of my voice, fighting to be heard over Radio One and Jigsaw's barking.

"Why don't you just listen to me for a few seconds?" Ross answered back, trying to keep calm.

"Why should I?" I yelled. "Why should I do what you say? Ever since Dad died you've tried to boss me around. Well not this time!" I screeched at such a pitch I nearly lost my voice.

"She's no good," Ross went on, telling me once more what he'd heard from a school friend he'd been talking to. Apparently, Louella had been running a bullying ring at our school before we moved here. She'd been forcing kids to buy cigarettes and stealing money from the First Years as well as landing them in all sorts of trouble with the teachers. The story was that she'd been expelled and gone to live with her uncle in America for a few months. But I didn't believe it. Talk about being far fetched, and I knew just how easily gossip got blown up out of proportion.

"I don't believe you, and I'm going to the party," I shrieked back. "You're just trying to spoil my fun and I'm not a kid anymore. I don't need looking after."

Sarah walked in on us and looked shocked to the bone.

"How can you argue at a time like this?" she said in a quiet voice that made me feel instantly guilty. Ross mumbled an apology and we stood with our heads lowered.

Then the phone rang.

"I'll get it," Ross said, moving towards the door.

"No, I will," I said, leaping forward.

"I'll answer it!" Sarah boomed from behind us.

We sat nervously waiting at the foot of the stairs while Sarah talked to James.

"What did he say?" I asked as soon as she came off the phone. My heart was practically in my mouth.

"Nothing showed up in the blood test," Sarah said. "Nothing at all, apart from her being slightly anaemic, but that's nothing serious."

"You mean, she's all right?" Ross asked, looking amazed.

"It appears so," Sarah said.

"No ragwort poisoning?"

"No."

"No liver damage?"

"No."

"That's brilliant!" Ross exclaimed, throwing his good arm round Sarah and grinning at me like a Cheshire cat.

"Yes, it is rather good, isn't it?" Sarah smirked, looking more like her old self.

"But if that's true," I said, coming back down

to earth with a bang, "if that's true, why won't she eat anything?"

Ross and Sarah looked blank. And the most awful thing was, none of us knew.

## Chapter Six

"I just don't understand it," James exclaimed, looking frustrated and at his wit's end. "There's no reason at all why she shouldn't eat. It's almost as if she doesn't want to. As if she wants to just slip away."

I looked at Queenie dozing in the straw and I had to agree. Her eyes had gone dull and lifeless and in the last three days she had shown less and less interest in what was going on. Even that morning she had barely noticed Danny go into her stable. Something was seriously wrong.

"What are we going to do?" I asked James, who had become almost a permanent resident at Hollywell over the last few days.

"I don't know," he answered, his soft dark eyes studying Queenie intently. "But I'm not going to be beaten. Queenie, you old girl, you're not going to give up on life yet. Not if I've got anything to do with it!"

He put the stethoscope back in his now familiar black case and turned to face me.

"Oh, no!" I groaned inwardly as I saw Danny's figure shift away from behind the stable door.

"What is it?" James asked, coming up behind me.

Danny turned and fled across the yard like a frightened rabbit, bolting for the hay barn.

"He must have heard everything," I said, wanting to kick myself for being so careless. My heart went out to the little boy whose pony was deteriorating more and more as each day passed.

"That's my fault," James blamed himself and went hurrying after Danny to explain. Or at least to try to make the truth seem a little less painful.

"Mel!" Ross bawled from the back door of the house with a cooking apron wrapped round his middle. The smell of eggs, sausage and bacon wafted into the yard and my stomach rumbled with hunger.

It was still early in the morning. Just gone half-past eight. The chickens we had recently been given by a neighbour had finally started laying and Ross had volunteered to do a cooked breakfast. I was just hanging up Sparky's old headcollar and thinking how the day promised to be blazing hot, when the postman came teetering up the drive on his old-fashioned Royal Mail bike. He handed me the post which consisted of a brown envelope from the electricity board, a letter for Katie from her pen pal in Australia and a white envelope marked for the attention of Mrs Sarah Foster.

I knew immediately who it was from. It had a London postmark, and in a corner the name of a best-selling book emblazoned in red letters. It was from Sarah's publisher.

"So this is it," I thought, running my trembling fingers over the stiff white envelope. Our whole future depended on what lay inside that letter.

I went over to the house, through the back porch into the kitchen like a zombie. I felt strangely numb from the feet up. I even had the wild idea of destroying the letter so we wouldn't have to face up to what it might say. But I knew that wasn't the answer. I had learnt a long time ago that you couldn't just run away from your problems. It only made them ten times worse.

Sarah was coming out of the washroom off the kitchen with a bag of cat litter under one arm and Matilda under the other. She was wittering away to Ross about something on breakfast television, but she stopped mid-sentence as soon as she saw the letter.

"I can't open it!" she shrieked, horrified, as I passed her the envelope. She flopped into the nearest chair and Matilda went diving outside with her coat stuck on end.

"Mel!" Katie yelled at me for leaving the door

open and went running after Matilda.

The letter had fallen to the floor and Jigsaw promptly pushed past and picked it up in his mouth.

"Don't let him chew it!" Sarah shouted, as pale as paper and incapable of standing up.

"I'll open it, all right?" Ross said, thumping down the knives and forks and taking the letter from Jigsaw.

"I don't want to know what it says," Sarah said, hiding her face in a nearby tea towel. By this time my heart was having palpitations and I just wanted to know, one way or the other.

"You've got it!" Ross yelled so loud I think the whole village must have heard. "You've got the job!" he went on, chucking the envelope in the air where it landed in the sink.

"I don't believe it," Sarah said, grabbing the letter and reading it word for word. "I honestly don't believe it!"

"What's all the racket?" Katie came back into the kitchen with a jittery Matilda, looking at us all as if we were crazy.

"We're saved!" I yelled at Katie, grabbing hold of her hands and dancing round and round. "We don't have to sell the field. We can keep the sanctuary!"

Tears were running down Sarah's face as she read the letter again and again.

"I don't think I've ever felt so relieved in my whole life," she said to Ross who gave her an enormous bear hug.

James walked in the doorway with Danny and looked instantly embarrassed.

"I'm sorry," he said and made to walk back out.

"Don't be daft," Sarah said, blinking through her smudged mascara and grabbing hold of his arm. "There's no need to be sorry for anything," Sarah explained, fresh tears cascading down her face. "Something incredibly wonderful has just happened," and with that James passed her a big white hanky and she blew her nose.

The rest of the day was like an ongoing party. James didn't have to go into work until evening surgery so he spent the day with us, clowning around and getting very little done. Katie and Danny were delighted and revelled in his jokes and pranks. It was almost as if James had become their father figure over night.

James went with Ross to the next village and bought a couple of bottles of sparkling wine and a bunch of flowers for Sarah, which didn't go unnoticed by any of us. We mixed the wine with fresh orange juice to make pretend Buck's Fizz, and Katie complained that the bubbles went up her nose.

Later in the afternoon, Mrs Mac came round and we made plans for the show. I felt so enthusiastic now, I was brimming with ideas for everything from the tombola to where we could hire a tent. Mrs Mac had already just about organized the whole event single-handed, and Monday morning we would put the advertisement in the local paper.

By teatime we were all slightly tipsy, mainly due to Mrs Mac's unexpected bottle of home-made cider. Sarah had fallen off her deckchair which caused peals of laughter. Jigsaw was walking around with a bright pink nose after dunking his head into somebody's strawberry icecream, and Mrs Mac was insisting we call her Gladys, which Danny and Katie deliberately picked up on as Gladioli.

Then it was time for me to get ready for Louella's party.

Ross and I had agreed to disagree on the subject, but his face still clouded over when he saw me go upstairs to get ready. Sarah told him not to be so stupid, and that someone had to go to represent the Sanctuary. Katie told him that Louella fancied him like mad which only infuriated him more.

Upstairs, I didn't have a clue what to wear. It

was supposed to be a barbecue followed by a disco and Louella had said to dress casual. In the end I settled for my best pair of jeans, trainers and a black Lycra top I had bought on impulse a few weeks ago. I smeared on a touch of coral lipstick and hoped Sarah wouldn't notice. Then I decided to go the full hog and caked on eye-shadow and black mascara. I was determined not to look out of place with all of Louella's friends. I only wished the "Luscious Lashes" mascara didn't make my eyes sting so much. Satisfied at last that I could pass for fourteen, I tiptoed down the stairs and bumped into James. Luckily Sarah was on the telephone, rabbiting away to someone from one of the local riding schools, and James offered to give me a lift which I gladly accepted.

Outside Louella's house there were cars everywhere. Expensive-looking Mercedes and BMWs pulling up, and teenage girls getting out wearing tight mini skirts and skimpy tops. They were shouting to each other in high-pitched voices and giggling hysterically at some shared joke.

I caught a glimpse of Louella's brother Patrick carrying a huge synthesiser with some of his mates. There were fairy lights everywhere and music blasting out from a marquee. I had no idea it was going to be such a big affair.

"Melanie!" Someone tapped me on the shoulder

and I nearly jumped out of my skin. It was Louella. She was standing with a red-headed girl who was wearing purple lipstick and looking me up and down as if I was a sack of potatoes. Louella looked sensational. She was wearing a black all-in-one suit decorated with sequins and her hair was all scraped back in a chic bun. I was beginning to think that nobody else had come in jeans. In fact, at that particular moment all I wanted to do was go home. Then someone pushed a glass of Coke into my hand and I noticed it was Patrick who was swanning round with two blonde girls, one on each arm.

"Where's Ross?" Louella asked in a cold voice. It had just dawned on her that I was by myself.

"He had a migraine," I lied, and knew it sounded pathetically unconvincing. Louella froze and looked as if she could have gladly punched me in the face.

"Well, of all the insults," she snapped, pursing her lips, and I realized Katie had been right all along about her fancying Ross.

"So the new boyfriend's not turned up?" The red-haired girl smiled lazily, looking like a cat playing with a mouse.

"Oh, shut up, Angela!" Louella hissed, her make-up starting to go shiny.

I decided to change the subject and told her

that we didn't have to sell the field. Angela nearly choked on her drink and Louella glared at me with eyes that I thought were going to burst into flames. She spun round and flounced off, nearly knocking a girl in stilettos flat to the ground.

"You've done it now!" Angela said, grinning as if something was funny.

"What do you mean?" I asked, feeling like a fish out of water and totally confused.

"Louella's dad was going to build her a house on that field for her eighteenth birthday. They've been checking out the planning permission for ages."

I could have fallen through the floor. So that was what it was all about. And this party was just a ruse to get together with Ross. Louella couldn't give two hoots about the sanctuary, or anyone else for that matter. I'd been taken for a complete and utter mug.

"Come on, let's get some grub," Angela said, grabbing hold of my elbow and steering me towards the outdoor arena where cooking smells were wafting around. I was in such a state of shock I couldn't speak. I found myself clutching on to a paper plate and nibbling at a sausage as I tried to regain my composure. Someone turned up Guns N' Roses even louder on the stereo and a lad pushed past me trying to pour a glass of beer down a girl's front.

What on earth was I doing here? I started to feel sick and dizzy, and I just wanted to go to bed. Patrick thrust yet another huge glass of Coke into my hand and I felt as if I was swimming.

"What's she playing at?" Angela said, looking across the arena towards the stables. Blake was leading Royal Storm across the all-weather sand, and Louella was strutting along at his side, carrying a riding hat. She shouted out in a voice that everybody could hear:

"Come on, Mel, it's time for your first riding lesson!"

Storm was all tacked up and prancing nervously. Blake kept his head down and his eyes averted. Suddenly the sausage in my mouth tasted like a piece of old leather. In my panic I accidentally stood back on a helium balloon and when it burst everyone turned round to look at me.

"Don't do it," Angela whispered to me. "She's just trying to make you look an idiot."

But my head was whirring round and round like a washing machine. I couldn't think straight. All I knew was that I'd had enough of Louella. I was sick of her little games.

"You're not chicken, are you?" Louella taunted,

as she held out the riding hat and her eyes bored straight into mine.

I did up the chin strap and moved over to Storm's side.

"For heaven's sake, Mel, don't be a fool," Blake hissed in my ear as I picked up the reins. He put his hand on my arm, but I shrugged it off. I was going to show Louella Fancy Pants once and for all!

I lowered myself into the saddle and felt Storm go tense. There was a streak of sweat down each shoulder and his ears were twitching back and forth. We moved off at a walk, his long stride eating up the ground. It felt incredible. I'd never been on a horse so powerful and well balanced. The saddle was so comfortable it felt more like an armchair, and slowly I began to relax.

I pushed him into a trot and revelled in his lovely soft action. I concentrated on my rising and sitting up straight. The people watching became just a sea of faces, all blurred together. I vaguely heard Louella's voice telling me to canter on, and I squeezed my inside leg on the girth and waited for a response.

What happened next took me completely off guard. He reared straight up, squealing in protest and flailing his front legs in the air. I clung to his neck like a monkey and tried not to look down.

For one awful moment I thought he was going to go over backwards and land on me. But then he seemed to remember I was still on his back. He lowered himself back to the ground, but stumbled badly, and I went flying off over his shoulder. I landed on the soft sand in a heap, but I wasn't hurt. My head just felt as if there were a thousand hammers thumping away inside it.

Blake came rushing up looking as if he'd just seen a ghost. He'd turned almost green. Louella's ghastly laugh cut through my fog and made me look in her direction.

"You're not up to much, are you?" She giggled in obvious delight. "Tell your mum to start you off on a donkey, or better still a rocking horse!" She laughed hysterically at her own joke, but no one joined in.

Blake turned on her.

"You spiteful cow!" he said in an icy voice. "You think you're so clever, don't you? You could have killed Mel with your stupid stunt. You silly, pathetic girl!"

"Hey, steady on!" Patrick said from a distance, swaying badly.

Louella was momentarily stung out of her senses, but then she lashed out her arm and slapped Blake hard across the face. Everyone gasped and started whispering among themselves. Blake didn't move a muscle.

"You're finished!" Louella threatened, in a stricken voice.

"Do what you like," Blake answered, "I don't care any more."

He lifted me up off the sand and led me to his flat above the stables.

"I should never have let you ride Storm," he berated himself as he poured out a cup of black coffee.

"Well, you did try to stop me," I said, picking the bits of sand out of my mouth and looking round the small loft.

"Look, there's something I'd better tell you," Blake passed me the coffee and pulled up another chair. "Oh, and by the way, Patrick's been spiking everyone's drinks with vodka, so that's why you feel dizzy."

"You mean I'm drunk," I laughed, gulping at the hot, strong liquid.

"About Lou," Blake went on more seriously. "Storm's tendons were badly swollen tonight through being over jumped. You noticed he'd got bandages on?"

I nodded my head.

"Lou knew he would do a mental if someone rode him, so she deliberately set you up. The lousy thing is I knew and I didn't stop you. I just prayed you wouldn't go any faster than trot. I was scared of losing my job and I didn't know what to do. But I made a right pig's ear of it, didn't I?"

His deep, intense eyes looked into mine, searching for something.

"Will you forgive me?" he asked, not breaking his gaze.

"Don't be daft," I answered, feeling slightly embarrassed. "I don't even blame you."

His relief seemed to spur off all his innermost worries. He started to tell me about Louella and how she abused her horses. How she whipped them and took away their food when they were naughty. How when he wasn't there she and Patrick used to rap Royal Storm.

"But that's illegal!" I said, my eyes bulging with shock and anger. I seemed to have sobered up in thirty seconds.

Rapping was a horrible practice of lifting up a pole so that it would hit a horse's legs just as he was clearing a jump. The idea was that it would make him jump higher next time, but it was a pretty cruel way of doing it. A person would stand each end of the pole and lift it up at the crucial moment. It terrified horses and ruined their confidence.

"Why didn't you tell somebody?" I asked Blake who was staring at his fingernails.

"Why indeed?" he said, looking sad and defeated. "A few years ago I got into trouble with the police. I was involved with a gang of lads who were stealing cars, only I didn't know anything about it. I was charged even though I wasn't guilty. Anyway, I lost the job that I had at the time in a show-jumping yard and I managed to get this one, even though I've got a record. But the chances of getting another one are zilch."

"But that's terrible," I said, truly horrified.

"I know," he said. "It's not very rosy, is it? And now I don't want to leave Colorado. God knows what would happen to him if I wasn't here."

I thought about the skewbald horse and how Louella didn't want anything to do with him.

"I wanted to tell you about this the other day," Blake went on. "When I was at your place, but I guess I lost my bottle."

"Ross will go berserk when he hears."

"Oh, but you musn't tell him," Blake said, looking at me pleadingly. "Not yet, not until I've worked something out."

"But we can't let her get away with it."

"I know, but first of all we need proof."

Blake rubbed his hand over his face and looked desperately tired.

"It's her mother's fault mostly you know. She puts her under so much pressure to win. Always nagging and pushing. Such a stupid woman."

I remembered the glamorous-looking woman in the swimming pool and later in the house when she was so patronizing to me and Katie.

"I couldn't believe it when I lost my old job," Blake went on, changing the subject and revealing some of his bitterness. "I was at one of the best show-jumping yards in the country and getting all the top rides. How could they even think that I was stealing cars? And then to sack me for it!"

"I'm so sorry," I said.

"Don't be," Blake answered, trying to raise a smile.

"It's just one of those things. What makes me laugh is that I've come out of a yard with forty top-class horses and the best horse I've ever come across is right here and nobody wants him."

"You mean Colorado?"

"Who else? That horse is one of the best jumpers I've ever seen. It's almost as if he's got wings."

I thought back to when we first saw him jumping that stone wall and realized it must have been Blake who came running across to catch him.

"Nobody knows," Blake said in a low voice. "But I've been secretly training him when no one's around. Lou's terrified of him. She's only used to horses that are already schooled for the job. She can't cope with a youngster. Colorado picks up her fear and goes off his head as soon as she comes near. I just wish I knew what she plans to do with him."

"But we must find out!" I said, a cold chill running up my back as I suddenly thought, "What if she sacks you?"

"Oh, she's threatened that before," Blake answered.

"She needs me as much as I need her. The last thing Louella wants is to have to find another button-lipped groom. Hey, look at the time, I'd better get you home."

Blake lent me an old oilskin to put around my shoulders and we tiptoed down the stairs. The music was still blasting out, but most of the party goers had gone home. There was just the odd figure dancing in front of the marquee or sprawled out on the grass. There was a nip in the air and I shuddered as we turned down the road into the blackness.

Outside our drive Blake stopped and said he wouldn't come any further.

"Remember what you promised," he said, looking intently into my face. "Don't say a word about Louella or Colorado."

"But—"

"No buts. I'll let you know what I plan to do. Just please do as I say."

And then he turned and was gone.

What plan? What could we do apart from report her? Surely it was best to tell somebody now, someone like Sarah who would understand. What was Blake playing at? I shut the gate with a clunk and stomped up the drive, itching with frustration. But I'd given my word. No matter what my better judgement, I couldn't break a promise. All I could do now was wait.

## Chapter Seven

"It's about Queenie," James said. "I've got an idea."

"It – it's nothing bad, is it?" Danny asked, petrified.

"No, course not," James reassured him. "But I've got an idea as to what might be wrong with her."

But he refused to tell us until Sarah arrived – he just asked Ross to bring Sophie in from the field, which only added to the mystery.

"What is it?" Sarah asked, minutes later, and just as curious as we were.

James took hold of the frayed leadrope from Ross and started coaxing Sophie into Queenie's stable.

"James, what are you doing?" Sarah asked, as Sophie's fluffy, short tail disappeared inside the doorway.

Queenie was lying down as usual – fiddling with some fresh grass that Danny had picked for her the night before and which she hadn't eaten. She looked up with her huge sad eyes, panicking for a moment as little Sophie bustled in all wide-eyed and gangly-legged.

"Come on, girl, look who's here to see you," James said in his most gentle voice, rubbing his hand on Sophie's neck and then letting Queenie sniff at his outstretched palm.

For a while Queenie didn't make any attempt to get up. She just stared at Sophie with dull, deadpan eyes and I could feel the disappointment racking through James as we all stood and watched in silence.

Then Sophie decided to make the first move. She sidled over to Queenie, squealing in her high-pitched, foalish voice and pawing the air with her long slender forelegs. A flicker of interest glanced across Queenie's old tired face. Quietly, James unclipped the leadrope and stood back, leaving Sophie free to roam round the stable.

Suddenly Queenie gave a deep, throaty snort and started struggling to her feet, pulling herself up with every ounce of strength in her body. She couldn't take her eyes off Sophie who was now exploring the back of the stable, picking at some soft meadow hay she had found in a corner.

"No, leave her," James said to Ross, as Queenie swayed violently to one side and stuck out her right foreleg to steady herself.

103

"Come on, girl, you can do it!" James urged, clutching at the leadrope and turning it round and round in his hands.

Slowly Queenie shuffled forward. She gently nudged Sophie's quarters with her speckled nose, sniffing her all over. Then she pushed her towards us like a mother with her foal.

"It's working," Ross said. "James, it's working."

Danny started crying unashamedly and ran forward to fling his arms round Queenie's neck. Sarah, whose bottom lip was quivering like a washing line gave James a huge hug and kissed him on the cheek which James fully appreciated and winked at Ross who couldn't stop grinning.

"So how did you know?" Sarah asked James later on while we were having breakfast.

Jigsaw was wolfing down the last of the burnt toast and somehow managed to shake his head so hard that frothy saliva flew everywhere and even splattered on the kitchen ceiling.

We had left Sophie in the stable with Queenie; they were getting along like long lost friends. Queenie's eyes were glittering so much Danny said they reminded him of Christmas lights.

"It's quite simple really," James went on to say, carefully wiping off Jigsaw's froth from the collar of his polo shirt. "I don't know why I didn't think of it earlier. I could tell by Queenie's udder and teats that she'd recently had a foal."

Danny nodded his head and said that James had asked him about it.

"Presumably it was just before Revhead got her," James continued, passing the margarine tub over to Katie. "That's probably why she fell so ill at Revheads afterwards, an infection must have set in. Anyway, I didn't think any more about it until I saw Sophie in the field the other day."

The telephone shrilled loudly from in the hallway and Sarah cursed as she got up to answer it. The rest of us were so enraptured with what James was saying we hardly noticed.

"So it suddenly dawned on me that she could be pining."

"What, for the foal?" Katie asked, smothering a muffin in two inches of blackcurrant jam.

"That's right, I bet it was either stillborn or taken away from her too early. It's my guess that she'd just given up on life."

"And seeing Soph brought her round," Ross said. "Gave her a reason to carry on."

"That's right. It's only because Sophie's not much more than a foal that it worked. Queenie's become her sort of foster mum."

"You don't think they're really mother and daughter do you?" Katie asked, suddenly pop-eyed and open-mouthed with her mega brainwave.

"No, definitely not," James laughed. "Now that really would be a fairy-tale ending!"

"And don't speak with your mouth open," Ross chided, as we got a first-class view of active tonsils and half-gorged muffin.

Sarah stormed back into the kitchen like a high-speed steam roller.

"That girl is the limit," she barked, flushing like ripened rhubarb.

"Who are we talking about?" James asked, thrown by the sudden change in conversation.

"Of all the arrogant, spoilt, stuck up, insolent . . . How dare she speak to me like that?" Sarah fumed from one end of the kitchen to the other.

The phone call had been from Louella Sullivan.

"She's only pulled out of sponsoring the horse show. Or she says her dad has. Says he's just been on the phone from New York and told her to tell me he's changed his mind. Load of codswallop if you ask me. She was lying through her teeth."

Ross groaned soulfully and sunk his head into his hands. "I told you we shouldn't get involved."

"Don't tell me I told you so," Sarah said, crashing the pots into the sink as if she was intent on breaking the whole lot. "Beggars can't be choosers, you said so yourself."

"Does this mean we're up the creek without a

paddle?" Katie asked. "Or is it a sail?" she added, slightly confused.

"It means we're going to find another sponsor from somewhere if I have to knock on every door between here and Land's End. And you, young lady, have got some explaining to do."

Sarah waved a two-pronged fork in my direction.

"Oh no," I groaned, wondering just what Louella had been telling her. But James saved the moment by subsiding into peals of laughter. He stood up and, going across to Sarah, started extracting the clean cutlery from inside the fan oven where she'd been carefully putting it away for the last five minutes. Then he picked up the tea cosy, which didn't look very much at home on top of the Fairy Liquid bottle.

Sarah glared at him for a moment with her jade green eyes and then burst into uncontrollable giggles.

"The joys of living with a writer," Ross mumbled. And I beat a hasty retreat to the stables while the going was still good.

That night James was to take Sarah to a special dinner and dance. By early evening she was as jumpy as a cat on hot bricks and totally incapable of deciding what to wear. All day long I'd been flying inside to answer the phone thinking it might be Blake, or running to the bottom of the drive every time I heard horses go past. He said he would get in touch but when would that be? I had kept my promise, not breathing a word about Louella, but it wasn't easy. I was sure Ross suspected something. He kept giving me curious sideways glances whenever he thought I wasn't looking.

By the time Sarah was ready to leave I felt completely exhausted.

"Guess what?" Sarah said, coming off the telephone and waltzing through the hallway. She'd just been sweet-talking the Managing Director of a local baby food firm into supporting the horse show. "We've got a new sponsor," she announced.

James walked in the front door looking resplendent in his black dinner jacket and bow tie. Sarah apologized and quickly dived back upstairs to change dresses once more. She came down looking even more ravishing in black taffeta which showed off her perfect shoulders and tiny waist. I had never seen her look more beautiful. James was truly stunned and said he would be the luckiest man at the dance.

After umpteen games of gin rummy and Monopoly which Katie and Danny won every time we collapsed into bed feeling ready to sleep for a week.

James and Sarah were due back about one o'clock. The house was in complete darkness. None of us had any idea what was happening outside.

The first we knew was when Sarah's voice came screaming up the stairs, harsh and ragged; desperate and scared. I sat bolt upright in bed and felt a cold wave of terror pass over me. Ross scrambled out of his room and bolted down the stairs. Sarah's voice drifted up from the hallway.

"Hello, is this nine-nine-nine? We're on fire. It's Hollywell Stables, sixteen, Russet Lane . . ."

Through the drawn curtains I saw the flickering yellow flames.

"James!" Ross was yelling as he disappeared into Fenella's stable and led out the trembling smoke-choked pony. The smell of burning was everywhere. A rafter came crashing down in the barn and more bales of hay burst into flames. The heat was intense.

"Where's James?" Ross shouted as I ran for the fire blankets in the feed shed.

"I don't know," I yelled back, frozen with fear.

Fenella, running loose and wild with panic, jumped over the small post and rail into the field and raced off into the safe blackness.

James surged out of Bluey's stable just as the

flames licked at the roof top. His dinner jacket was wrapped over Bluey's head so he couldn't see the fire.

"The barn's about to come down," James rasped, the smoke dragging at his lungs. "There's still Queenie and Sophie."

I heard Sophie's high-pitched neigh coming from the stable in the corner. The fire was spreading from the barn through the stable block. James grabbed the fire blankets from me and belted off with Ross. Bluey stood dazed and shaking and I couldn't get him to move away. I tugged at his mane and screamed at him, the black smoke stinging in my eyes and mouth. The noise from the flames was deafening, but all he kept doing was shaking his head where the fire had singed his ears.

"Come on, will you!" I yelled, choking with desperation and lack of air. The barn started to collapse and the flames shot up another ten feet in the air.

Suddenly, I had an idea. As light as a rabbit I vaulted up on to Bluey's old bony back. Praying it would work, I closed my bare legs round his sides and dug in my heels. Miraculously, he seemed to wake up from his trance and moved forward. I kept him going until we reached the field gate where he went through and joined Fenella and Sparky.

Back in the yard, Sophie and Queenie were stumbling around with their heads between their knees and their eyes deadened with horror. Sophie was clinging to Queenie's side and the wise old pony made a beeline towards me, keen to get her little friend to safety. Sophie gangled after her, still neighing in panic, her gentle eyes ringed with white.

Fire engines wailed down the lane and I saw the flashing blue lights turning up the drive.

"Oh, no!" James said, and ran off to where Sarah was standing dangerously close to the dis-integrating barn, holding up a fire extinguisher which looked pathetically small against the blazing holocaust. The torn, soiled taffeta dress was hit-ched up round her knees and she was shaking con-vulsively, screaming angrily at the leaping flames.

James reached her in three bounds. He threw the extinguisher to one side and swept her up into his arms, carrying her back to safety just as the last joist of the building finally gave way.

The fire-fighters were everywhere, pulling out the long web hoses and talking to James and Ross.

"Leave it!" James said, pushing Ross back from the fire. "You've done enough." He wrapped a blanket round Sarah's shoulders, his own face stream-marked with smoke and sweat. "There's nothing more we can do."

We stood by the huge red fire engine and watched the firemen set to work with their hoses. I saw Katie and Danny staring out of a downstairs window where they had been told to stay. The fire licked and spat over the roof of the stables, ravaging the rafters and hungrily devouring as much in its path as it possibly could. One of Sarah's carefully arranged hanging baskets crashed to the ground and lay broken and shattered.

"We're ruined," Sarah mumbled, distraught and broken herself, burrowing her face in James' shoulder, unable to watch the destruction any longer. High up in the clear blackened sky a galaxy of stars winked and shone, serene and unaffected, a long, long way away.

Sarah put one arm round my shoulder and another round Ross and surrounded by burning wood and the acrid smell of smoke, we stood and looked out on our shattered haven. In such a short time our whole life had been turned upside down. All our plans wrecked. What should have been a perfect evening for Sarah had turned into a worst nightmare. Huge jets of water now pounded into the heart of the fire, but it was too late. Much too late. The damage had already been done. All we could do now was pick up the pieces and work out how and why?

## Chapter Eight

It was arson.

There was no doubt about it. The police found a petrol can under the charcoaled debris of the barn. Whoever it was hadn't even bothered to make it look like an accident.

Sarah was livid when she heard about Bazz's visit and subsequent threats. She couldn't understand why we hadn't told her, but even if we had, who'd have guessed something like this was going to happen?

The police were very interested in our story and came back with the news that Bazz had disappeared. Nobody had seen him since yesterday afternoon and Revhead was refusing to comment.

Ross was stomping around in a temper because Sarah wouldn't let him go off to find Bazz.

"Well, it's obvious he's the one. What are the police doing about it? What's anyone doing about it?"

"He could be dangerous," Sarah insisted and I was inclined to agree with her. I could still picture that ugly, pulpy face with the narrow, drawn mouth and the evil glinting eyes. It terrified me to think that he'd come so close to our ponies – and while we were just a few feet away in the house.

Later, Blake called round on Royal Storm after hearing about the fire from the local shop-keeper. He was aghast when he saw the barn and stables completely gutted. He couldn't understand why nobody had seen anything.

"About this Bazz character," he said guardedly, unsure whether to continue. "I don't know for definite, it might just be coincidence, but I'm sure I saw his black and gold bike outside Louella's last night."

There was a weighted pause as we all tried to absorb what Blake was saying.

"What time was this?" Ross asked.

"Late, very late. I'd just come back from having a drink with a mate in town. It must have been gone midnight."

The atmosphere tensed with buzzing brains as we all started to put two and two together.

"But how does she know Bazz?" I asked, perplexed.

"It would fit." Ross ignored me, his eyes as dark as elderberries and shining with anticipation. "If our place was burnt down she might think we'd be forced to sell the field. It's also a good way of getting her own back."

"But nobody would be that nasty," Sarah said.

"We know Bazz is," Ross added.

"No, it's too ridiculous for words," Sarah went on. "There's no way someone like Louella would be involved with a person like Bazz. And besides, being spoilt and petty is one thing, being an arsonist is totally another."

"It wasn't her who struck the match," Ross answered.

"I don't care. This isn't going to get us anywhere. Let the police handle it. For all we know it could have been any half-witted hooligan passing by."

It seemed ages before Blake and I were finally alone together and I could ask him about Colorado. I had suggested putting Bluey in the field as an excuse to get out of the house and Blake had immediately volunteered to come and help.

"So what's happening?" I asked as soon as we were out in the yard.

"You haven't told anyone have you?" Blake said, looking pensive.

I shook my head.

"I think Lou's going to change her ways," Blake said. "She's admitted as much and I think we ought to give her a second chance."

"Are you serious?" I asked, shocked at Blake's sudden change in attitude. "What's she been saying to you?"

"Nothing, I just think we ought to see if she means it. Besides, I asked her about Colorado."

"And what did she say?"

"Only that she's going to put him in the sales this autumn, that she's not bothered how much he fetches, just as long as she gets rid of him. Don't you see, I've got to save up enough money to buy him. I can't let him be sold for meat or go to some crummy ignorant owner. I've got to hang on to my job long enough to get the cash."

Poor Blake. I didn't know what to say. Colorado meant everything to him. His shoulders seemed to have dropped six inches and he looked so lonely and defeated. At least when I had troubles my family were there to share them with me. What must it be like to have no one?

"Correction," I said, putting on my most authoritative voice. "Until *we* find the money."

Blake looked up in surprise.

"And I don't want any lip," I went on. "If you don't let us help you, I'll, I'll . . ."

"You're certainly no chicken are you?" Blake butted in, flashing me a cheeky grin.

"Huh, I'll give you chicken," I said, picking up the hose pipe that was filling up the water trough.

"No, mercy, mercy," Blake cried, as I sprayed water all over him. He told me that I was a hard woman, and then Ross, who must have come out of the house without me noticing, sneaked up behind me and chucked a bucket of water over my head.

"You rat!" I yelled and whipped around with the hose just in time to catch Mrs Mac full on the chest with a jet of icy water.

"I'm so sorry," I gasped as Mrs Mac picked at the sodden blouse that was now clinging to her mountainous bosom.

"Melanie!" Sarah roared in her extra stern voice from the yard where she was turning off the hose pipe.

Blake shook his wet hair like a hairy dog and said it was partly his fault. Water was still dripping off the end of my nose. Luckily, Mrs Mac didn't take it to heart. She said she didn't like the blouse anyway and set about recruiting Blake to help with the horse show which we had already done earlier.

"Eight thirty a.m. sharp," she was saying. "This Saturday, and remember to bring your wellington boots. The forecast's for showers."

The rest of the week was chaotic. With a lot of painstaking effort, Ross and James managed to haul a tarpaulin sheet over two of the stables to form a make-shift roof. Luckily, they were brick-built so we still had four walls. Unfortunately, the barn hadn't fared so well – in fact, there was nothing left, including all the winter hay which we had bought with some of Sarah's money. I had no idea how we were going to cope.

Sarah had been wrangling with the insurance people until she was blue in the face. They wanted to know all about how the fire started and even intimated that we might have set up the fire ourselves so that we could claim the money. Of all the cheek. It could be months before we received a cheque and then we would have to wait for a new roof to be built. I had visions of our ponies huddled together in the field with no shelter and the snow, wind and rain lashing into their faces. James was trying to keep us in good spirits and was making enquiries about renting some unused cattle sheds in the next village. Ross put his mountain bike and his Sony stereo up for sale but it would be just a drop in the ocean.

Sarah meanwhile, was locked in her study for most of the time working on her new novel. She said all the upset had stimulated her creativity so at least something good had come out of it. James couldn't understand her craving for banana yoghurt, so we had to explain to him that writing always gave her these strange obsessions. Last time it was oven chips and before that it was pickled onions.

Queenie was doing superbly and by Thursday evening James announced that she was well on the way to recovery. Mrs Mac had roped in more helpers for the show than she knew what to do with. Even the Vicar had been ear-marked for the tombola. The baby-food firm came good with the sponsorship and on the schedule we had names like Riley's Rusks novice jumping class, Riley's Gripewater working hunter for ponies. It was hilarious but it certainly created the desired interest with the local riding schools and pony clubs. The local paper even did a preview on their sports page which delighted Mr Riley so much that he made a donation to our sanctuary of one hundred pounds.

The police were still trying to track down Bazz without success, and when they questioned Louella she denied having anything to do with him. But of course she would.

By Saturday night everything was supposed to be under control and it was, except for the dark clouds looming up from the west. There was nothing like rain to dampen a show's profits. Mrs Mac however kept the sun shining in the house with her endless enthusiasm and energy. She had even managed to get a mechanical bronco horse and a children's trampoline to add to the highlights. Katie and Danny were adamant that Sparky was going to win the jumping and the fancy dress. Danny had taken to riding like a duck to water and Katie was a bit put out that he could already jump higher than she could.

When Sunday morning dawned blustery and cold I brushed off any doubts and set to with the preparations.

"Mel, Mel, where're the rosettes?" Sarah screeched up the stairs as I was scrubbing my teeth.

"Under the television," yelled Ross who was trying desperately to get the loudspeaker to work. Three of the villagers were in the kitchen doing the catering. They were so busy gossiping they didn't notice Jigsaw running off with most of the egg and watercress sandwiches. Katie was sulking because she couldn't open her birthday presents until the next day.

"Why wasn't I born on a Sunday?" she was complaining. I left Ross to answer that one and made a quick exit through the French windows.

Outside a couple of tents were billowing in the wind and a caravan was being positioned by the main ringside. The local saddlery shop had brought a stall and was busy setting out everything from headcollars to mucker boots.

By a quarter to ten everything was just about ready. The loudspeaker was blaring out some old country and western music which Ross promptly changed to Tina Turner.

Mrs Mac was too nervous to notice and it certainly livened up the tempo.

"Oh no!" she burst out as the first car and pony trailer bumped its way on to the field. "Where's the judge?"

Sarah came running out of the house right on cue to say the show judge was stuck in a traffic queue on the motorway coming back from a week in Cornwall.

"That's all we need," Mrs Mac puffed. "Oh, well, James will have to step in. Now where's he got to?"

Beefburgers and tomato ketchup wafted in the air as black clouds gathered over the field.

"Where's the toilet?" a little girl in pigtails asked me, dripping a chocolate ice-cream all over her clean jodphurs.

"Where is everybody?" Sarah said at nearly half-past ten when the only people who had turned up were two girls who had hacked from the next village, three trailers and one horsebox.

"It's a bit cold, isn't it?" one of Mrs Mac's less

substantial helpers was complaining. The poor woman was trembling like a leaf and looking for her cardigan which I had a sneaky feeling had disappeared a short while back in Jigsaw's mouth. By eleven o'clock Mrs Mac was getting desperate.

"Where is everybody?" she shrieked as we looked down the empty drive and expected to see a convoy of trailers at any minute. The rain started coming down in huge plops and pinging off the caravan and fragile tents.

"When are we starting?" Katie rode up on Sparky whose plaits resembled inflated golf balls. I was beginning to get seriously worried.

"Maybe they don't think it's until the afternoon," Mrs Mac suggested, trying to keep hopeful.

"Maybe they don't think it's started at all," said Ross, whose face was blacker than the looming clouds.

Blake was busy handing out coffees in the refreshment tent where everybody seemed to be huddling. He looked as worried as I felt. The rain was getting steadily heavier and thunder rolled close by. James abandoned the main ring and ran for cover.

"This is ridiculous," Sarah said, finally deciding at a quarter to twelve that enough was enough.

"I'm going to find out what's happened."

"And I'll come with you," Mrs Mac said, who

was fast wilting into a state of despair. They headed back to the house to ring the local riding schools and the Pony Club secretary.

"I don't believe it," Sarah was frothing at the mouth a few minutes later. Mrs Mac was dabbing at her eyes with a pretty lace hanky.

"They all think it's been cancelled," she bellowed out in a voice that must have echoed round the whole county. "Someone rang round last night to say it was off, it seems that they contacted just about everybody in the area."

"You mean it's been sabotaged?" gasped James, ignoring the rain that was pounding down on his unprotected head.

"Without a doubt," Sarah said. "And I bet you a week's washing-up I know who's behind it."

"Louella," Blake murmured from behind the tea counter.

"But why?" Mrs Mac blubbered, heartbroken that all her good work had fallen apart.

"Because she's a nasty stuck-up little cow and I'm going to give her an earful," Ross exploded in a fit of temper.

"That's just what she wants you to do," Sarah said. "If we do that she'll only gloat and pat herself on the back."

"Well, I'm not going to sit back and let her ruin our lives!" Ross yelled out.

"Are you sure it was her?" I asked Sarah.

"Positive. Mrs O'Neil said it was a girl's voice. Who else could it have been?"

Doom and gloom hovered over everyone's heads like the black plague.

"Now, look here," barked a big man with a black beard who came across leading a cream-coloured pony, "this show's a shambles. Is it on or off?"

"Off," Sarah snapped, as the heavens opened with great sheets of driving rain. "Definitely off," she repeated and I felt like shoving a sodden tea towel down his throat.

We sat in the kitchen drinking tea in a state of shock. Poor Katie's bottom lip was so low it could have touched her knees. Even James was stuck for what to say. Mrs Mac was inconsolable.

"Well, there's got to be a bright side," James said, unable to stand the gloom any longer. "Imagine if the Vicar had been wearing a wig, or if that beefcake with the beard had bopped me on the nose. And it's not as if the tents blew down, and, just think, we can live off caramel slices and cheese and pickle sandwiches until the cows come home."

Sarah threw her slipper at him.

"What cows?" Danny asked.

"Well, how does this grab you?" James said. "A trip to the pictures, followed by hamburgers and chips and as much ice-cream as you can eat?"

"Yeah!" Katie yelled, her eyes spinning round like Catherine wheels.

"And you as well, Danny," Sarah said, as Danny looked unsure if he was included.

Half an hour later, dressed up in their best togs, Katie, Danny, Sarah and James set off in the car with Katie half hanging out of the window waving frantically at Ross and myself. We had decided to stay behind to keep an eye on the ponies. We didn't want a repeat of the fire or any other nasty surprise. Besides, there was still a lot of clearing up to do!

"Here, catch!" Ross said, throwing the dish-cloth straight at me and then sitting down and helping himself to caramel slices.

"You can dry," I protested, looking at the mountain of washing-up piled in the sink. I still couldn't believe how spiteful Louella had been. To have gone to so much trouble to ruin our show. "She must really hate us," I said to Ross who was busy feeding Jigsaw the last of the egg sandwiches.

"It's her upbringing," he said after some thought. "She's been so spoilt she doesn't know any better – she's always been used to getting her own way and the first time she doesn't, she can't handle it."

"All I know," I said, anger building up inside me, "is that she's ruined our only chance of raising some money. And if we can't take in any more horses because we can't afford to feed them . . . it's all her fault!"

By the time we'd cleared up and given the ponies their evening feeds, we'd both had a chance to cool down. James and Sarah turned in the driveway looking tired but happy. Danny and Katie were holding silver balloons out of the window, which got caught up on the holly tree. The sun was setting like a plump orange in the west and grey shadows trailed over the lawn like long fingers. The last throws of Happy Birthday spilled out into the balmy evening and I suddenly realized that despite all our troubles at least we had each other. We were a family and somehow no matter what it might take, we were going to keep Hollywell Stables running.

# Chapter Nine

There it was again.

I was lying in bed with the duvet up to my ears, nervously listening to a rapping noise at the window. The alarm clock pointed to one thirty-four a.m. The whole house was dark apart from the bathroom light which glowed in the hallway.

Help! There it was. Rat-a-tat – rat-a-tat. Sharp, shrill, as if someone were throwing small stones at the window. Oh my goodness, that was it! Some-one *was* throwing stones at the window. The hairs at the back of my neck stood up like a porcupine. What was I going to do?

Don't panic. Keep calm, be brave. Take a deep breath. I stuck a foot out of bed and peeled back the duvet. All had gone deathly quiet. Maybe who-ever it was had disappeared. I sidled over to the curtains, clinging to the wall for protection. Inch by inch I edged closer. A pale pink moon illumi-nated the driveway in soft shimmering rays.

Down below I saw a shadow move and then

step back again. Another stone pinged off the window and I jumped back in alarm.

"Mel," a man's voice hissed.

I felt my blood run cold.

"Mel, it's Blake, where are you?"

Relief surged through me and I rushed frantically to open the window.

"Blake," I whispered, "what's happened?"

A few minutes later I was fully dressed and creeping out of the house as stealthily as a burglar. Blake was waiting in the orchard at the front, half hidden among the trees.

"What's the matter?"

I caught my breath when he turned round. His face was drained stark white against his black hair; his lashes wet and a look of stricken anguish etched into every crevice of his face.

"Mel, you've got to help me, it's Colorado."

Quickly we moved along the deserted road towards Louella's house, keeping well in the edge and out of sight, Blake revealing the whole story.

Louella had come back early from a party and caught him schooling Colorado on the all-weather arena. She had been eaten up with jealousy and temper at the way Colorado was jumping a huge upright and parallel bar. She gave Blake the sack on the spot and told him to be out of his flat by the morning. Then she grabbed at Colorado's reins and was knocked backwards as he reared up. She wasn't hurt but she made a point of laying on the ground pretending to be concussed. Her mother came running out, screaming her head off and Louella insisted Colorado had attacked her. Mrs Sullivan said he was obviously dangerous and later that afternoon she rang the vet and ordered him to come out the next day. They were going to have Colorado destroyed.

At this point Blake was so distressed, he could barely get his breath.

"I'm not going to let it happen, Mel, no way."

Colorado was in a stable round the back of the main yard. Blake's plan was to smuggle him out and hide him somewhere nobody would think of looking. We didn't have much time and Blake's suggestion was perfect. At the far end of our five-acre field in a small dip near a wood was a broken-down shed that was big enough to hide Colorado. It couldn't be seen from the road and most people didn't even know it was there. We had no time to lose.

Louella's house was in darkness as we crept across a back field towards the stables. Colorado whickered gently as he saw us approaching.

"Ssssh boy, keep it down," Blake whispered, as Colorado kicked at his door a couple of times with impatience.

Silently, we pulled back the bolts and crept inside. The smell of woodshavings and new hay was overwhelming and at least gave me a sense of familiarity. My heart was hammering and I knew what we were about to do amounted to nothing less than kidnapping.

I nearly jumped out of my skin when a tabby cat with no tail dived out of the manger and ran off into the night. I was clutching Blake's arm so tightly my fingers ached.

Colorado was nervous at first, but soon settled down when I offered him some oats out of my coat pocket. Blake did up the headcollar and took hold of the leadrope.

"If we keep him on the grass," he whispered, "nobody should hear anything. The secret is not to panic."

Luckily we were far enough away from the house not to be noticed; if it had been the main stable block it would have been a different story.

Blake led Colorado out into the cool night air. The horse's ears were pricked straight ahead and he looked strangely mysterious as the moonlight flickered on his brown and white coat.

"Going somewhere?" a voice spoke up behind us.

It was Bazz.

My heart did a triple somersault. Blake stopped

dead in his tracks and slowly turned round to face him.

"So this is where you've been hanging out. I might have guessed."

Colorado snorted and started edging backwards into a privet hedge. Blake thrust Colorado's lead-rope into my hand, never once taking his eyes off Bazz. Somewhere near the main house a dog yapped and I thought I heard a door open.

"You're not stopping us," Blake said, "so you might as well crawl back under the stone you came from and forget you saw any of this."

A flicker of doubt edged into Bazz's face. I could see he was having second thoughts about taking on Blake. He took a step backwards, fumbling in the darkness, his face half in the shadows.

Colorado, oblivious to what was happening and already bored, pulled hard on his rope trying to reach some unmown grass and unwittingly stood on my toe. In the moment that Blake was distracted, Bazz grasped hold of a pitchfork that must have been leaning against the stable wall. He waved it in front of him, his face suddenly lighting up with a chill malice.

"Gotcha now," he grunted, the two metal prongs glinting in the moonlight.

Blake stood stock still, not moving a muscle.

"Well, come on, then," Bazz goaded, flickering

the fork at Blake until I could hardly watch anymore.

Bazz's mouth tightened into a narrow line when Blake refused to rise to the bait.

"Yer a coward," he said, edging the fork closer to Blake's face. Still Blake didn't move.

Bazz stepped closer and held the prongs just inches away from Blake's eyes.

I didn't know what to do. Colorado was yanking me all over the place and sweat was pouring off me. Blake just stood there immobile and as cool as a cucumber. But Bazz was starting to crack under his steady penetrating stare. He laughed nervously and lowered the fork down to Blake's mouth, almost grazing his nose with the pointed prong.

"Put it down, Bazz," Blake said in a level, threatening voice.

"Why should I?" Bazz answered, the fork shaking even more.

"Because if you don't I'm going to break your neck."

Doubt flickered in Bazz's face.

"Remember last time you tried to take me on," Blake growled menacingly.

For a few seconds they both eyed each other like battling rams and then Bazz's face crumpled in defeat and he let the fork drop to the ground.

"You can take that nag for all I care," he grunted, "That cow Louella can do 'er own dirty work from now on."

"Now listen, Bazz," Blake said urgently, "we're getting out of this place with this horse and you're not going to say a word to anyone. Got it? Because if you do, the police will be down on you like a ton of bricks. And if I were you, I'd stop letting that brother of yours and every other Tom, Dick and Harry push you around."

Bazz backed off, nodding his head up and down like a chastised child. We made our getaway before he changed his mind, picking our way through the long grass in the back field which would eventually lead us on to the road. Colorado, happy to be on the move at last, settled down and walked along at my side. We didn't want to move too fast in case we caused a disturbance but on the other hand we had to put as much distance between us and the house as quickly as possible. It was hard to see where we were going and I kept brushing into thistles which felt as prickly as cactus.

"You were incredible back there," I said to Blake and really meant it.

"I was shaking inside," he admitted, "but I just figured that all bullies are cowards at heart."

We came up to a narrow wooden gate and went through on to the road. A car whizzed past exceeding the speed limit and with their lights on full beam. Nerves fluttered in my stomach as I wondered if Bazz had broke the news.

"It's nobody," Blake said, reading my thoughts, "Just some oaf coming back from a party. Come on, let's go."

We moved forward down the road clinging to the grass verge and wishing now that the moon wasn't so full.

"If we can just get to the end of this road," Blake said, "we're home and dry."

Colorado suddenly dug in his heels and stood staring at something in the hedgerow.

"What is it?" I whispered to Blake, hardly able to stand any more nerve-wracking surprises in one night.

"A fox. There, look, jumping over that wall."

I just caught sight of its brush disappearing into the darkness. Overhead an owl hooted and I heard its wings flapping.

"Here," Blake said, stopping at a well-worn track leading into the woods. "If we go down here we can paddle through the stream and get into your field that way. Save us being spotted on the road."

Colorado wasn't too keen on the wood, seeing dragons lurking in the shadows, and it took us ages to get him into the stream even though it had practically dried up. Thank heavens Blake was there because I would never have had the nerve to do this by myself. Everything looked so different at night and there were so many strange noises. It was like entering another world.

"There it is," Blake said, as what was once an old cattle shed loomed up out of the darkness. Part of it had been knocked down so there was only enough room for one horse. We were never sure how safe it was so we kept it shut up until we could afford to rebuild it. Now I was worried sick about Colorado staying here. It was obvious we'd have to find somewhere else to put him tomorrow, or rather today – it wouldn't be that long before the sun came up.

"Don't worry, Mel. This will do for now. Anything's better than Colorado being shot."

And I couldn't argue with that.

I left them both huddled together in the musty dampness, Colorado enjoying some oats Blake had brought for him. I set off back to the house before anyone noticed I was gone. Blake had sworn me to secrecy believing that if Sarah found out she would feel she had to send Colorado back. But how was I going to keep something like this a secret? It was like asking the Pope to stop praying. I just knew the truth would come out and when it did, what then? All I was sure of was that we couldn't let Colorado die and I had enough faith in Sarah to know she wouldn't let that happen.

Just a few hours later Louella pounded into the yard on the Wizard, practically grinding her teeth in white-hot fury.

Sarah was coming out of the chicken hut with the fresh eggs and Ross was emptying a barrow of dirty straw from the stable. I'd just been to see Blake and Colorado on the pretext of taking Jigsaw for a walk. Somehow I'd managed to sneak out with some cheese and bread rolls and a couple of packets of salt and vinegar crisps. Nobody suspected anything and Sarah, spotting the black rings round my eyes just assumed I'd had a restless night.

Now, as the Wizard skittered in the drive while Louella dismounted, my stomach tied itself into tight knots and I wished somebody would "beam me up" into outer space. Louella's white hair was flying all over the place as she flounced over to Sarah screaming, "Where's my horse?"

Sarah looked as if someone had just hit her over the head with a brick.

"I beg your pardon?"

"You heard me, it's no good playing games with me. I know what you're up to. Now where's my horse?"

Louella's eyes were flashing like red-hot coals and her whole lithe body was shaking with pent-up anger.

"How dare you think you can get away with it!" she shouted like a spoilt brat. Her face flushed as red as her lipstick and a muscle twitched constantly in her left cheek. I had never seen her so angry.

"Give me back my horse!" Her voice echoed all round the yard causing Jigsaw to tremble with his tail between his legs. I felt very much the same way.

Ross was marching across to her looking as though he was about to commit murder. Louella, desperate for a reaction from Sarah who just stared at her like a zombie, grabbed hold of the fresh eggs in their cardboard tray and crashed them to the ground. Yellow yolk and cracked shell splattered over the tarmac and half way up the Wizard's forelegs. The poor thing stood there shuddering with nerves but unable to move because Louella was gripping his pelham bridle so tightly it was crossing his jaw.

"That'll teach you to mess with me," she yelled, and flounced off to look in the stable and the paddock for Colorado. Sarah, suddenly coming out of her trance, chased after her.

"Leave this to me," she snapped to Ross. She caught hold of Louella's shoulder and whipped her round. "Get out!" she shouted, her red hair clashing with her reddened face. "Get off this property before I drag you off by your split ends. Do you hear me?"

Louella's jaw dropped open.

"I've had it up to here with you," Sarah went on, stoked up like a steam engine. "What with pulling out of the show, sabotaging the entire event, nearly putting Mel in hospital. Who on earth do you think you are?"

The colour was draining from Louella's face so fast she'd turned an unpleasant shade of magnolia.

"Now, get out before I report you to the police. And grow up for God's sake, before someone sticks a dummy in your mouth."

Ross started slowly clapping his hands together in applause. Louella was so embarrassed her eyes bulged like a bullfrog's.

"You're not getting away with this," she squeaked, tears watering her mascaraed eyes. "I know you've stolen Colorado . . . just wait till I tell my dad."

She sniffed loudly and rode off on the Wizard who looked as if he'd much rather have stayed behind.

"What was that all about?" Ross asked, as peace settled back in the yard and Jigsaw lapped up the broken eggs as if it was his lucky day.

"That girl gets worse," Sarah said, cooling off and trying to make sense of Louella's accusations.

"Mel, do you know anything about this?"

"What?" I jumped, turning round in the process of sloping off to the house. I have never been very good at telling lies.

"Mel, what's the matter? You've turned purple!"

"Yes, Mel," Ross said, "you've been very quiet."

"N-nothing," I stuttered, squirming under Sarah's probing eyes.

"I'll, I'll j-just go and make breakfast," I said, feeling as if I was about to be kebabed.

"Melanie."

It was a losing battle.

"You know we don't keep secrets in this house," Sarah said, pronouncing each word very slowly.

"W-we didn't have a choice," I stammered, feeling outnumbered two to one. Even Jigsaw was looking at me accusingly.

"W-well it was like this . . ." I said. And the whole story came flooding out.

# Chapter Ten

"I'm sorry, Mrs Foster, we should have told you." Blake bumbled with his head hung low as we stood in the kitchen weighing up the situation.

"Too right you should have told me," Sarah, her eyes on stalks, marched up and down with a hen feather still stuck to her back.

Colorado was in the stable munching at some pony nuts and hopefully keeping a low profile.

"Do you know how much trouble we could be in?" she said, swivelling round on her heel and nearly tripping over a cat-nip mouse.

"I'll take all the blame," Blake said, looking worn to a frazzle. "It was all my fault, not Mel's."

"Oh, no, you won't," Sarah boomed, and then immediately softened. "Because I would have done exactly the same."

Blake's face flushed with relief.

"What we've got to do now is work out a plan of action," Sarah continued.

"I've been thinking about that," Blake brightened, hope at last invading his shattered face. And he went on to tell us in every detail just what he'd got in mind.

"Wow," shrieked Katie and Danny in unison.

Sarah nodded her head thoughtfully.

"But will it work?" I butted in, terrified that it would backfire in our faces – after all, it was a very long shot.

"There's no other choice," Ross said grimly. "It's either this or send Colorado back . . . It's *got* to work."

"Let's go for it," Sarah made up her mind, slanting her green eyes in gritty determination and touching Blake's shirt sleeve with her long artistic fingers. "It's all down to you, Blake," she said.

And so we put the first stages of our plan into action.

"Where's the ashtray?" Ross shrieked, diving into the kitchen, clutching a Hamlet cigar which had dropped into a vase of water.

Sarah was putting out the best tea service on a silver tray and banging all the cupboard doors looking for the brown sugar.

"I'm running out of things to say," I felt as though someone was tugging at my nerve ends like pieces of elastic.

In the sitting room, Mr Sullivan, Louella's father,

was sitting on our rose-patterned sofa drumming his fingers on the arm rest and no doubt wondering what was going on. Sarah had telephoned him a few hours earlier and organized an urgent meeting for three o'clock and now all she could do was witter on about the weather and the local comprehensive school.

"Where *is* Blake?" we all whispered together as our carefully laid plan started falling apart at the seams.

"Don't panic," Sarah said. "We can handle this, just keep him talking, Mel."

Keep him talking, keep him talking, I mumbled over and over as I went back in the room with the ashtray and a box of matches. Mr Sullivan was standing up looking at a photograph on the mantelpiece of Ross and myself both on Sparky.

He wasn't a bit like Louella. Nobody would have guessed from the way he talked and dressed that he was so rich and powerful. I hoped he would see our side of the story.

Colorado was hidden well out of sight but every now and then I was sure I heard him neighing to Queenie who was mothering him like a fussy old nanny. Katie and Danny were sat upstairs with their fingers and toes crossed for good luck, strictly forbidden to come down until it was all over, just in case they let the cat out of the bag.

"Please, Blake, turn up soon," I prayed in desperation as the grandfather clock ticked heavily in the corner and there was still no sign of him.

Sarah bustled in, clattering the tea tray and looking about as uncool as a sausage in a sauna.

"I really can't stay long," Mr Sullivan said, looking at his watch and sitting down again. Sarah reeled off into a conversation about vegetable growing, something which she knew absolutely nothing about.

I was just about to give up hope completely when Blake burst through the door followed by an elated Ross grinning from ear to ear. A video tape was tightly clutched in Blake's hand.

"I've got it," he said, and Sarah looked as if she'd just been saved from the guillotine.

"Blake?" Mr Sullivan mouthed, looking dumbfounded.

"I'll explain later," Sarah answered hurriedly slotting the video tape into the recorder and pressing "Play".

The television flickered into life with a snowy, crackling picture. What if Blake hadn't filmed it properly? Then the picture righted itself and there was a clear shot of Louella's house and the stable yard. Then Louella cantering Royal Storm round and round the outdoor arena.

"What is this?" Mr Sullivan demanded, clearly annoyed and confused.

But then his eyes fixed on a shot of Louella's brother Patrick standing by a jump and another lad holding the opposite end of a pole. The picture faded a little but it was still possible to see. Louella was slowly cantering up to the jump and just as Storm was airborne in a lovely arc, Patrick and the other lad rapped up the pole so hard that it clouted Storm full on his forelegs with a nasty crack.

"Got you!" Sarah winced, clenching her fist into a cushion balanced on her knee.

Mr Sullivan's face had set in a stony mask.

The video ran on showing Louella jumping again and again until Storm was so frightened that he was clearing the fence by a good two feet. Patrick was laughing and Louella looked well satisfied. Only Storm was a bundle of nerves, the sweat dripping down his neck in streams and his eyes rolling with terror.

"Switch it off, switch it off," Mr Sullivan mumbled, wiping the palms of his hands on his trousers, his face white with shock.

"I'm sorry we had to do this," Sarah said, pressing the remote control and turning off the television. "It was the only way we could save Colorado."

"I beg your pardon?" Mr Sullivan looked even more confused than before.

"You mean, you don't know?" Sarah asked.

The poor man didn't know anything. He was horrified when we told him about Colorado. He also swore that he knew nothing about the rapping.

"I just earn the money," he said, his face desolate with embarrassment.

"W-what will you do?" he asked, stroking little Matilda who had somehow sneaked in and was kneading her claws on his lap.

"That's up to you," Ross said, "but we were going to send a copy to the BSJA and the RSPCA."

"And if I promised you none of this would ever happen again. What then?"

Ross looked at Sarah.

"What if I gave Colorado to the sanctuary and agreed to pay for his upkeep?"

My eyes shot forward on extendable springs.

"Come again?" said Ross who obviously thought he was hearing things.

Blake collapsed into a spare chair like a sack of potatoes.

"Are you serious?" Sarah asked unbelievingly.

"It seems the best solution to me," Mr Sullivan went on. "Louella can't do a thing with the horse, if we sell him he'll end up in a meat yard. At least here he'll be safe."

"What about the other two?" Blake asked.

"Oh, I guarantee they'll be properly looked after. No daughter of mine is going to behave like that." He glanced over at the video with a look of disgust. "I promise you I won't go back on my word."

As Mr Sullivan's Mercedes saloon swished down the drive, Sarah squeezed my hand so tightly in hers my fingers went white.

"We've done it gang," she said, unable to contain herself any longer.

"Yee-hah!" Ross whooped like a cowboy, flinging his arms round Sarah and swirling her off her feet. I couldn't stop grinning. Katie and Danny came charging out of the house with Jigsaw bounding ahead.

"We heard everything!" Katie shrieked. "We were listening outside the door!"

Later that afternoon we had a phone call from the police to say that Bazz had been picked up at his house collecting some clothes and he'd been taken in for questioning. Mrs Mac and Sarah had gone out to buy supplies for a celebration party and James was calling round after evening surgery. Ross and I were still interrogating Blake on just how he'd managed to clinch the video.

"Of course, I always knew everything would

work out," Mrs Mac was saying to James as she perched on the edge of the sofa. At least with Sarah's cheque we would be able to survive until Christmas and after that we would just have to come up with another way to raise money.

Sarah went to fetch the remains of Katie's birthday cake which was made in the shape of a horseshoe. I devoured a Jaffa cake and Ross read bad jokes out of a Christmas cracker, only it wasn't Christmas.

"I just can't believe Colorado's safe," Blake was saying over and over. Sarah had made up a bed for him in the spare room and he was staying with us for the next few weeks until he decided what he wanted to do.

"I wish I could stay here for ever," Danny said wistfully, feeding a cheese and pineapple square to Jigsaw.

Outside the horses were enjoying an extra dollop of molasses and sliced carrots as a special treat. Looking down at Danny reaching for another Chocolate Fudge it was hard to believe he was the same little boy we had found crying on our doorstep. He'd blossomed every bit as much as Queenie and it was hard not to think of him as part of the family.

"These are the best summer holidays ever," Katie said, turning on some music. "Just think of all those ponies out there just waiting for us to save them."

"Oh, no, Katie, not 'Nelly the Elephant' again."

"So, just how did you get that video?" Mrs Mac asked Blake who was passing round the chocolate fudge.

"Quite easily, really. I managed to borrow a camcorder off a friend of mine and hid in the trees until Louella came out. I had a feeling she was going to try something because there's a big show coming up next week. I had to wait until Mr Sullivan had left though – she won't try anything while her dad's there. That's why I was so late getting back. At one stage I thought the recorder had broken."

"Who's eaten all the marzipan?" Sarah came into the room carrying the cake in one hand and a bottle of sparkling wine in the other, with a party hat balanced perilously on top of her head.

James passed round the glasses and proposed a toast to Hollywell Stables.

"Hear, hear," we all shouted as the cork flew into the air with a giant pop.

"Hip, hip, hooray!" Danny yelled as we clinked glasses and Blake turned up the stereo which was playing "We Are the Champions".

"All's well that end's well," James whispered in my ear and put an arm round Sarah's shoulders.

For the first time since Dad died I felt like a whole person again. Closing my eyes for an instant I sent a special prayer to all the ponies all over the world who needed us. They were the champions I thought, ponies like Queenie and Sophie and Bluey – so brave and gentle and trusting. I didn't know what the future was going to bring but I felt on top of the world.

"Come on, Mel, you're missing it!"

Everybody had spilled out into the moonlit garden and was doing the Conga round the apple trees.

"Look!" Danny shouted, pointing at the sky. "A shooting star!" But at that moment I couldn't think of anything in particular to wish for. If happiness truly was "contentment of the soul" then yes – I was happy.

# Hollywell Stables 2.

## The Gamble
Samantha Alexander

*Hollywell Stables – sanctuary for horses and ponies.
It was a dream come true for Mel, Ross and Katie . . .*

It was a gamble. How could it possibly work? Why should one of the world's most famous rock stars give a charity concert for Hollywell Stables? But Rocky is no ordinary star and when he discovers that the racing stables keeping his precious thoroughbred are cheating him, he leads the Hollywell team on a mission to uncover the truth . . .

Praise for Hollywell Stables:

'Hollywell Stables is the vanguard of the new breed of pony stories . . . these are cracking stories.' *TES*

'The action comes thick and fast with adventure after adventure rolling off each page.' *Riding Magazine*

# Hollywell Stables 3

## The Chase
Samantha Alexander

*Hollywell Stables – sanctuary for horses and ponies.*
*It was a dream come true for Mel, Ross and Katie . . .*

Emotions run high at Hollywell Stables when the local
hunt comes crashing through the yard. The
consequences are disastrous, and Charles Stonehouse is
to blame.

Then one of the sanctuary's own ponies goes missing.
Could the culprit be Bazz, who is back on the scene and
out for revenge? The Hollywell team know they have to
act fast: there's no time to lose . . .

# Hollywell Stables 4

## Fame
Samantha Alexander

*Hollywell Stables – sanctuary for horses and ponies.*
*It was a dream come true for Mel, Ross and Katie . . .*

Rocky's new record, Chase the Dream, shoots straight
into the top ten, and all the proceeds are going to
Hollywell Stables. It brings overnight fame to the
sanctuary and the family are asked to do television and
radio interviews. On one show they get a call from a girl
who says she has seen a miniature horse locked in a
caravan, but she rings off before telling them where it
was. The Hollywell team set off to unravel the mystery . . .

## Riders 1

## Will to Win
Samantha Alexander

*"Alex Johnson, I'll never understand you. You own a horse with a reputation for being a complete maniac and you think you can waltz into your first competition and win."*

*"I don't think," I threw back at her. "I know."*

Alex Johnson is a girl with one burning ambition: to become a champion three-day eventer. The only thing distracting her from her goal is the gorgeous Ash Burgess, who runs the yard where she keeps her horse . . .

# Riders 2

## Team Spirit
Samantha Alexander

*"It's crazy." I stared down at the list of team members for the Pony Club One-Day Event. "It's got to be a mistake!"*

*"It's true." Zoe came off the phone. "Apparently it's a lesson in public relations. We've all got to learn to get on, team spirit and all that."*

Alex Johnson and her arch-rival Camilla Davies have been put on the same team for the Pony Club One-Day Event. Will they be able to forget the past and form a winning team?

# A selected list of titles available from Macmillan and Pan Books

The prices shown below are correct at the time of going to press. However, Macmillan Publishers reserve the right to show new retail prices on covers which may differ from those previously advertised.

SAMANTHA ALEXANDER

HOLLYWELL STABLES

| | | | |
|---|---|---|---|
| 1. Flying Start | 0 330 33639 8 | £2.99 |
| 2. The Gamble | 0 330 33685 1 | £2.99 |
| 3. The Chase | 0 330 33857 9 | £2.99 |
| 4. Fame | 0 330 33858 7 | £2.99 |
| 5. The Mission | 0 330 34199 5 | £2.99 |
| 6. Trapped | 0 330 34200 2 | £2.99 |
| 7. Running Wild | 0 330 34201 0 | £2.99 |
| 8. Secrets | 0 330 34202 9 | £2.99 |

RIDERS

| | | |
|---|---|---|
| 1. Will to Win | 0 330 34533 8 | £2.99 |
| 2. Team Spirit | 0 330 34534 6 | £2.99 |
| 3. Peak Performance | 0 330 34535 4 | £2.99 |
| 4. Rising Star | 0 330 34536 2 | £2.99 |

All Macmillan titles can be ordered at your local bookshop or are available by post from:

**Book Service by Post
PO Box 29, Douglas, Isle of Man IM99 1BQ**

Credit cards accepted. For details:
Telephone: 01624 675137
Fax: 01624 670923
E-mail: bookshop@enterprise.net

**Free postage and packing in the UK.**
Overseas customers: add £1 per book (paperback)
and £3 per book (hardback).